To Darren
with love

Do Dogs Think

AND OTHER CRESCENT VALLEY SHORT STORIES.

Keith Field

Mam xxx
&
Keith Field

Published by:

FriesenPress

Suite 300 – 852 Fort Street

Victoria, BC, Canada V8W 1H8

www.friesenpress.com

Distributed to the trade by The Ingram Book Company

Acknowledgements

A special thanks to Althea McElheron for her helpful suggestions in revising, her rewriting of certain scenes and co-authoring of Wait and See.

Fiction
by Keith Field

What is fiction other than the segments of an author's life?
Stored in a jumbled disarray through which he must shed some light,
But when he writes his fictitious tales, he's told that they aren't true,
Yet he'll place these segments in such a way that the truth in life shows through.

FREE FALL
*BASED ON TRUE STORIES
HAPPENED AT VANIER IN
'69, 1 YEAR AFTER I GRADUATED!
MOM

Table of Contents

Do Dogs think?

Well the whole thing began simply enough. These kind of things usually do. It was one of those hot muggy afternoons of mid June. We were sitting on the back porch drinking beer and killing mosquitoes, my wife Joan and myself. I was watching the chickens scratching amongst the quack grass in the backyard. We have some Barred Rocks and Leg-horns. Elmo, our combination, Lab, Setter, Retriever, was lying on his burlap sack at the top of the steps sleeping. His toes were twitching and his mouth was flapping and he was making some grunting noises like he was trying to run and bark. Back when I went to school, they taught us that animals couldn't hash things out. But Joan was telling me that when people wiggle like that in their sleep they're rehashing their day. I got to thinking about that. I think about crazy things like that when I've been sitting a while. At least, my wife thinks they're crazy. Like what good does it do, she'll say. No good, I guess. But that's not why I do it. Now take those chickens. They can see two different scenes at once, a different one out of each eye. Now take us. We can only see straight ahead and concentrate on one thing at a time. Just try it. You'll see. Now think about this. Can a chicken concentrate on the two different scenes at the same time or does it have to switch its attention back and forth? Anyway, my wife, Joan, she was laying back in one of those lounges that you can buy real cheap at one of those Big Box, stores in the Crescent Valley Mall. I mean she looked real nice laying there snoring. She's a nice looking woman; no kidding; shapely; long red hair. She acts nice too. You'd like her. She jumped when the phone rang. We have one of those remotes. I didn't want to get one of those damn things because you can hear them ringing but you can't find them. But the wife, Joan, she wanted to buy one and so that's what we did.

It was sitting right between us on the old card table. She made a grab for it. Normally she would have got it but I guess she hadn't got woke up properly yet because she knocked all the depleted cans of Crescent Valley Lager off the table. One rolled straight for Elmo's nose. When it made contact, it gave him quite a start. The rest clattered down the steps and scattered the chickens. I picked up the phone.

"Who?" I asked. It was a guys' voice I'd never heard before so I said all this to him, "No. A Joan Hawkins does. Who is this anyway? What do you want? If you're selling we're not buying...yes, she used to be a Martin, but not now. She's a Hawkins, my wife...yes, that's right, she is...yes, I know I am...look that's all fine and dandy but who the hell are you and how did you get this number?"

Joan pulled on the sleeve of my T-shirt and asked, "Is it for me? Is it for me?"

I leaned away a little so she couldn't quite reach the phone and I continued to talk to this guy. "You have ways? Look fella., don't play games with me. Who are you?...Her 'X'...I didn't know she had an 'X'...now isn't *that* the news of the day, eh?"

"Give me the phone if it's for me," Joan said.

So I told her it was for a Joan Martin. That she's Joan Hawkins. Then I said to the guy, "Look fella, just forget about your 'Xs' and your 'Os' and move on."

Joan yanked the phone from me and gave me a look. "Hello, is that you Erin?" She said this in a voice that didn't sound at all like her. "Yes, that's right...I got married two years ago...oh he's just a little touchy. Sure I'm happy. How about you?...is that right....yes...yes...why of course, drop right over....oh no, no, no, of course not. He won't mind at all...yes, you turn left off the freeway on the Mosquito Creek access road. About ten kilos and you hang a right...that's the Old Crescent Valley road. We're another ten or so kilos out. You'll see the mail box...F. Hawkins...just follow the lane to the old farm house, that's us...you too...see you in a while...bye now."

"Your 'X'?" I said. "He won't mind? Who won't mind? What won't he mind?" I said all this calmly enough but then I raised my voice a little to make sure she could hear me. "What in the hell is going on, Joan? You never told me you were married before."

She gave me kind of a funny look, got up, opened the screen door and walked into the kitchen. I followed her, scraped a chair out from the kitchen table and sat down. She went over to the fridge and opened it. Her voice was very quiet when she said, "I wasn't." Reaching into the fridge, she lifted out a plastic container of tonic water. "We just lived together for six years."

'What's the damn difference?' I didn't *ask* this but it went through my mind.

Without looking at me, she walked over to the cupboard and took out a 1.75 litre bottle of gin and a couple of glasses. "Like a G and T?"

Then I knocked my voice up a notch and said, "Six years, Six bloody years you lived with this guy and you never told me about him. Six bloody years…yes, yes, sure, I'll have a G and T. Maybe I'll have a half dozen of the buggers."

Joan turned from the sideboard where she was pouring the gin, and said, "So what's the big deal…he's just an old friend…now…I don't know why you're so upset."

"I'm not upset," I said. I guess just because I was talking loud, she thought I was upset.

She turned back to mixing the drinks, but of course, kept on talking. "I'm sure you had girl friends that I never heard about."

"Not any that I lived with for six years," I let her know. Funny but I remember I was wearing the T-shirt that I bought down at the store on the crossroads. It had 'Where The Hell is Mosquito Creek', printed across the front. I remember cause I looked down at the beer stains on it cause it was sticking to the sweat on my chest and I was pulling at it. "So how did he get your…*our* phone number, eh?" I asked her. "Tell me *that*…if he didn't know your married name…that's a puzzler, eh?" I teetered my chair on its back legs and gave her a look, cause I figured I had her there.

"How would I know?" That's all she said. "How would I know?" then she walked over to the table and set the drinks down, one in front of me. It slopped on my T-shirt but I didn't care. Like I said, it had beer stains on it. Then she scraped a chair into place. Once she had sat down, she just looked straight across the table at me with one of those looks of hers, took a sip of her gin and said, "Ask him yourself when he gets here. He phoned from the convenience store. He'll be here within a half hour."

I waited a while to think of something to say. Finally I said, "A half hour, eh?" But I was really thinking, *'Six years, eh?'* Then I scuffed my feet on the old linoleum floor and tapped the edge of my glass on the oilcloth. I don't know. For some reason I just couldn't relax. It was like I had so much to say but couldn't think of any of it.

Joan was looking down at her gin when I said, "I hope he has no intention of staying because if he does he's in for a surprise."

This made her look up pretty quick. "Oh, don't be silly, Floyd. What's past is past. Water under the bridge."

'More like dirt under the carpet,' I almost said.

"I don't know what you're so upset about. Look, would you do me one favour? All I ask of you as my loving husband is this, will you do me just one small favour?"

I looked out the window. There was couple of jays squawking and pecking at each other in the apple tree. Neither flew away. They just kept at each other. I kept my eyes on the birds when I asked, "What?"

"Be polite and nice to him," Joan said. Can you believe that? She said, "Make him feel welcome…at home."

'But he isn't welcome…he's not at home.' Of course, I never said this. I just thought it. What I really said was, "I don't understand why you have to see this guy."

"That's all I ask…for the short time he's here." Joan laid her hand on mine while she said this. It *did* feel nice all right.

Anyway, I said to her in a stern voice, "It better be."

She just gave my hand a little pat and said, "Please dear…for me."

I mean, Joan has a way with her. So I thought for a while and then I said, "How would you feel if I dragged some old flame of mine in here? Someone you had never heard of before? Someone I had lived with for six years?"

Then without batting an eye, she said, "I'd have no problem with that at all." Funny, but I think she actually believed it.

So I said to her, I said, "You split up with this guy, didn't you? So why do you want to see him? I don't ever want to see hide or seek of any of my "Xs"."

"Nor tail," she said.

For a sec I didn't know what she meant but then I picked up on it and said, "Oh yeah, hide nor tail." Then I went on. "The point I'm trying to make is that when you split up with someone you should never want to see them again, ever."

"But you loved them," she said. "…supposedly…at least at one time, you did. You can't forget that."

When she was saying all this, she got this look on her face. You know how a person will be saying something then as they are saying it they will start to listen to what it is that they are *really saying* and wonder about it. Well, anyway, I said to her, "I can. No problem." Then I rapped my glass hard on the table. A little harder than I meant to, I guess. Not that I didn't have a good enough reason to rap it as hard as I wanted to. After all, it *was* my wife who had been involved in this…uh, *situation*…that we were discussing… and it *was* my table I was rapping on…well our table. Anyway, I said, "I hate their guts. I forget every descent thing that happened between us… if any descent thing ever did. I never want to see hide or…nor tail of them again, ever."

Then she runs this one by me. "The very fact that you feel so strongly against them now, shows you still have feelings for them. If you didn't, you would feel completely indifferent as to whether they were around or not."

Last year she took a psychology course at one of these adult learning classes. You know the kind. They have them at night in some school room and they talk about all these things that are supposed to be going on in a person's head that he doesn't know about but make him do things that he doesn't want to do, or shouldn't, and they try to see who can come up with the best guess as to what's going on in this guy's head. Sort of like one of those guessing games people will play at a booze party, except in this case no one knows the answer. Anyway, sometimes when we have these little discussions some of this stuff will come out. So when she said all this, I thought that it could have been some of it coming out, but I wasn't sure if that's what this was or not. I needed time to think, so I asked, "Could you run that by me again?"

So she tries to explain. "What I'm saying is that if you no longer have any feelings for them…no remnants whatsoever of that love you once felt, then you should feel indifferent toward them."

"But I do feel indifferent," I said. "I hate their guts."

So she tells me that that isn't indifference; that indifference is not feeling anything at all. Not even hate.

Now I was *sure* that this was coming from those classes, so I toyed with my drink for a while to think this one over, then I asked, "So how do you feel about this guy?"

At this point, she got this soupy look on her face and when she talked she seemed to be looking across the field at the barn except the wall was in the way. "When I think of Erin, I think of the good times only. Of course there were trying times as well. There always is…but I don't regret them. I learned from them. It's just that I prefer to dwell on the positive aspects of our relationship…the good times."

She didn't quite sell me on this, so I said to her, "Well, if you learned from the bad times, you should have learned to stay away from him?"

Then she looked at her glass as if she was talking to it instead of me. "He brought happiness into my life for a time. We owe our 'Xs' something for that, don't we?"

I took a while to think about this notion too. Finally I asked, "How long ago was it that you lived with this guy?"

She peered over her glass at me. It was pretty empty by then. Then she said, "Oh let me see now. After Erin there was that car salesman…then that newspaper reporter…of course, there was the school janitor…after that the hippie and…well let's just say some miscellaneous husbands…so, that would have been, Jeez…nine or ten years ago."

'Hippie…let's just say, Jeez is right.' Of course, I just thought this. What I said was, "I just think we should all forget about the past."

"Well, I think *both* of us owe Erin something for the past happiness he gave me."

"Both of us!" I yelled. I don't remember exactly what I said right after I yelled. I guess I was too mad. Just something to do with how did I get into the picture and that I didn't owe him a damn thing and that I didn't care who he made happy. I must have said something wrong here because she said, "What? You don't care if I was happy then?"

So I told her that I didn't know her then. How can someone care about someone they don't even know?

"But *now*…we're talking about *now*…you want me to have been miserable when I was with Erin."

Now this didn't make any sense at all, so I said, "How can I care if a woman that I didn't even know at the time was happy because of some things that some jerk did for her and be grateful to this jerk for doing these things when I wouldn't even know him if I saw him on the street and when I don't have the foggiest idea of what they were anyway and when they were over and done long before I ever met her and of course too late for me to do anything about them if they hadn't made her happy? It's impossible."

She studied me with this frown for a sec, then she said, "No it isn't."

So I told her that it already happened so it was too late to feel anything about it. Then she just sat there for a bit shaking her head at me with this puzzled look on her face, then she said, "You know, Floyd, you're not making any sense at all."

Of course, I was making plenty of sense, but I decided back off a bit so as not to aggravate the situation anymore than I had, so I said, "The important thing to think about here is 'right now'. That's where it's at, eh? Like 'right now'. And right now, I want you to be happy...and right now, I'm always doing things to make you happy, eh?"

"But you didn't want me to be happy before you met me...hm, of course you couldn't have because you didn't even know me then...Cripes, now look what you've gone and done. You've got me thinking your crazy way. Now give me a minute to get this straight...now I've got it. You want me to be miserable so *you* could have been...no, that's not right...You wanted me to be miserable so you could come along and make yourself happy by being the big hero. That's it...isn't it?"

You know how something will be so simple but you just can't seem to get someone else to understand what you're getting at? Anyway, I thought it would be a good idea to go back over the last few things we'd said to sort of clear up a few odds and ends. There was something that wasn't coming off quite right here. I looked through the screen door at Elmo. He got to his feet and sauntered over. First he looked at Joan and then at me. His tongue was lolling out of the side of his mouth and dripping. He slid it in and turned and walked back to his sack. Finally I said, "I don't get it. I mean, what more could a woman want than to have a husband who does all sorts of things to make her happy? Hundreds of women would give their right leg for a husband like that."

"Right arm," she said. "But you want to be the one who does it."

"Of course, I'm your husband. I have every right to want to make you happy."

"But you do it for the wrong reasons. You do it to make your*self* feel good."

"Sure it makes me feel good. What's wrong with that?"

"It's selfish." She said. "Don't you see? You're doing it for yourself…to give yourself the pleasure of making me happy."

"What's wrong with that?" I asked her. "You *are* happy, aren't you?"

She didn't answer for a second, then she said, "Sure I'm happy. But I want you to try to make me happy because you want me to be happy…not because you want to make yourself happy by making me happy."

This too, could have been from that psychology course, but again, I wasn't sure. I needed time to think so I didn't say anything for a long time. When I figured I had the right angle worked out, I asked, "Don't you want *me* to be happy?"

"Of course, but not by making me happy."

Now I wasn't at all clear on how I was going to make her happy and be miserable myself but I figured I better do something to get the conversation going in a different direction so I suggested that I fix our drinks and that we go sit on the back porch again. So we did that. But there was something about the whole thing that didn't make sense to me, so I asked, "So if this guy made you so happy then why did you split?"

"He threw his clothes on the floor and put his feet up on the table."

"Judas Priest!" I said. "What a dastardly thing to do." Then I laughed. I guess this was a mistake because *she* didn't. She just looked at me kind of funny and said, "Oh there were other minor problems." At this point, she seemed calm enough.

So I told her that there were in any relationship.

"Yes, I'm aware of that," she said. "…but you know how minor problems can escalate sometimes….into misunderstandings of greater consequence."

I knew about this, so I nodded.

"…like how one thing will lead to another, eh?"

I nodded.

"…then all it will take is one incident…one bloody incident and…and the whole…" It was right about here that Joan raised her voice a notch. "Do you know what the bugger did?"

I told her that I didn't.

So she got to her feet still holding her glass. I figured she did this so she could better explain it to me. "This…this girl that I had gone to school with dropped into town. I mean, we weren't close friends in school. It was just that she was in my class. So she phones up and wants to visit. So what could I say? I said okay. But when she comes she says her husband kicked her out and she has no place to stay. I mean, I never even liked her in school. But Erin said sure. Stay as long as you like." Joan's face was getting a little flushed at this point in our talk. "Do you know what happened then?" she asked moving over to where I was sitting.

I told her that I didn't. So she leaned forward to tell me.

"Next day I went to work. Erin didn't have a regular job. He was an artist…wasn't painting though. He was waiting for inspiration. So I got off work a little earlier than usual. I worked as a barmaid and sometimes things were slow. Anyway, when I got home there was no one around so I was about to go into the bedroom and Erin walks out with this weird expression on his face. I thought, 'Good. He's inspired', but then I noticed that he was doing up his pants. So I asked him where the girl was. Just then she came walking out buttoning up her blouse."

Then Joan pointed her glass of gin at me and in a shrill accusing voice, she said, "So I asked them what the hell was going on? He said they were just talking." Joan shook her glass in my face and said, "Can you believe that? He expected me to believe that? Can you believe that?"

I shook my head. She moved her face closer. I could see the pupils of her eyes plainly now. You know how a person's pupils will dart about when they are looking for something to throw or someone to hit?

Then Joan yelled, "Do you *really* want to know what he did next?"

I didn't but I yelled, "What?"

"He grabbed her." Joan grabbed my shirt. "And *kissed* her. Can you believe that?"

"Yes!…No!…Yes!" I yelled.

"…right in front of me. I mean, like *really kissed* her, eh? Eh?"

"Eh!" I yelled as I tried to free my T-shirt from her grip. Then she let go and swung around facing the yard and yelled to someone out there that I couldn't see. "So I told him, 'I'm history, you bastard and I never want to see your face again'. Then I picked up a can of beer that was sitting on the table and threw it at him."

Joan used her glass of gin instead of a can of beer to demonstrate this point but it didn't really matter. The way she fired that glass across the yard,

I had no problem getting the picture. It hit the concrete side of the well and flew in a million pieces. You should have seen the chickens scatter. What a fuss. Feathers flying everywhere. Elmo raised his chin from his paw and watched Joan slowly turn and sit down. He had a look on his face like a person will get when they watch an ant carrying something too big for itself. Then he laid his chin back down on his paw. After that I didn't say anything. Joan didn't say anything either. You know how it is sometimes when you've been talking about something for a long time: like you feel you've said everything you can say about something and there's nothing more to say? Anyway, we sat there a long time. All you could hear was the odd whine of a mosquito and slap of a hand. After a while, there was the sound a car pulling off the main road and crunching along the gravel of our lane. I guess Joan could hear it too. It was loud enough. Elmo didn't bark. Then the crunching stopped at the front of the house. You could just make out a car door click shut. Then there was the faint sound of what could have been sandals scampering up the front steps. Then there was some knocking. We sat there for the longest time just listening to this knocking. It got louder before it stopped. Then there was the sound of what could have been sandals slapping their way down the steps. A car door gave a loud 'thwack' just before a motor revved and there was the sound of what could have been gravel flying about. A few minutes later, there was the sound of a car taking-off in the direction of the main road then quickly getting fainter and fainter and fainter until you couldn't hear it anymore. I looked at Elmo. He lifted his head and looked at me, panting. You know how it looks like a dog is laughing when it's panting? After a while I got to wondering; 'Do dogs think?'

Down to the Sea Again, on BC Ferries

If you are that elderly lady in the flowered hat poking your nose up against the windshield of your '62 Country Squire as you wait in line for the Horseshoe Bay Ferry on your homeward journey to Victoria on this balmy autumn afternoon, you might be wondering at the lack of decorum in the proceedings.

If you are that officer in your Taurus, sitting with brow pleated two cars back, anxious to arrive at the military base in Crescent Valley on schedule, you might question the irregularities involved.

If you are that truck driver leaning against the fender of your 'semi' waggling a toothpick in your teeth, you could be a tad rankled at the delay.

But if you are one of the newly weds in your Corsica three cars back on your way to your honeymoon at Flopping Flounder Inn, it's quite likely you can while away the time with preliminaries.

And who is this individual standing before his trailer with hitch in hand, a radial saw, jointer, toolbox and mattress, secured to its warped wooden box with a frayed rope and towering above the conveyance like the Vancouver skyline. He's clearly no vagrant, not with the neatly pressed pleats of his beige slacks flapping in the breeze as he steps up to the tollbooth with all the dignity of a Legionnaire parading with a flagpole in his navel.

"What are *you*…ah…meant to be doing, sir?" the young lady in the tollbooth asks.

"Doing?" he asks. "Why I'm simply standing in line waiting to buy a ticket for Departure Bay." He smiles pleasantly as he sets the hitch down on the Tarmac and reaches for his wallet.

"But you're standing on your feet."

"Why of course I am," he says, with that tone of wisdom that one frequently associates with teachers. "How else is one to stand?"

"But it classifies you as a foot passenger."

"Then I'll sit on the hitch tongue."

She points across the lane of ferry traffic. "You should be getting your ticket inside the waiting room over there."

"But my luggage wont go up the stairs," he replies, with that pleasantness that comes with years of teaching children.

"But that's not luggage."

"Well, what is it then?"

"It's freight."

"Can you tell me what the salient features are that differentiate luggage from freight?" the possible teacher asks.

With both hands providing support from the sill, the girl states firmly, "Why…there *must* be a difference…I mean, there *is* a difference."

"Yes, but can you give me the correct answer?"

"Let me see now," she says. Suddenly, she raises her hand.

"Yes?"

"Portability," she states emphatically. "Luggage must possess portability."

"Can you give me the correct definition of the word 'portability'?"

"You can lift it."

The teacher clears his throat and corrects. "The correct definition for the word 'portability' is (cough) that which can be carried and/or transported."

"Easily."

The teacher looks down and coughs at the implications before stepping over to the booth and placing a knowledgeable hand on the sill. "Now, let's stop and consider that point for a moment. What about those large suitcases you see people pulling through air terminals? I doubt that they can lift all of those…ah, easily."

"Yes…well…of course there *are* exceptions to every rule."

"In that case, wouldn't you say that my situation should be classified as an exception? I mean really now, how often do you see someone pulling a trailer in your ferry line-ups?"

"Never…until now."

"Point in case, now why don't you just measure my trailer and we can get on with proceedings?"

"What's the hold up," the truck driver yells from the running board of his rig.

The girl at the booth throws a smile at him that disintegrates on its way. "We have a situation here, sir. There'll be an *unavoidable* delay."

Digging deeply into her authority, she comes up with, "You simply *can not* tow that trailer onto the ferry by yourself."

"Why not?"

"Because that trailer and its load will be too heavy for you to pull up the ramp at Departure Bay."

"Nonsense! Its gross weight doesn't exceed five to six hundred pounds at the outside. And…" He picks up the hitch to demonstrate. "…as you can see, it's well balanced. Besides there's always someone around who can help push."

The truck driver gets into his rig and slams the door. A horn honks. Another honks. A chorus of honks.

"Will that gentleman with the trailer please remove it from the premises?" resonates across the parking lot from the control tower. This causes a crowd of curious travelers to step from their vehicles onto the tarmac.

"Look," the teacher says. "Since this seems to be a problem with you, why don't you phone your superiors?"

She grabs the phone and dials. "We have a…ah, a *situation* here, you see…" After her explanation to her 'superior', there is a brief period of silence, then turning to the teacher, she says, "My 'superior' says that we no longer transport stage coaches, covered wagons, mule trains or any other *animal* drawn conveyances."

"Animal! I'll have you know I'm *not* an *animal*."

The crowd applauds, although one can't be sure which side of the concept the crowd is in agreement with.

"Sorry sir, but he was simply making a generalized…"

"What about rickshaws?"

Again the crowd applauds.

"What about rickshaws?" she asks her superior. Then speaking to the teacher, she states, "He says we have never had the occasion to deal with rickshaws but…"

"Tell him he has now."

More applause.

"Would the man in the beige slacks please remove his trailer of junk from in front of the toll booth; he is holding up traffic," resonates across the ferry terminal only to bounce harmlessly off the teacher's smile as he turns to bow graciously to the crowd.

Then the toll girl says, "My superior requests that you kindly pull your trailer off to one side to allow for us to continue our operation as a public transportation facility and that he will talk to you *personally* on the phone after you do that."

Pleased that co-operative steps are being taken, the teacher pulls his belongings to one side and goes to the booth. The girl hands him the phone and turns to attend to the elderly lady in her Country Squire.

"Some people!" the elderly lady says to the toll girl as she hands her a credit card.

"Yes," the teacher says into the phone. "That's how the matter stands at the present time…no, you see, I have no vehicle…on this side, that is. My wife is driving it down Island from Crescent Valley to meet me at the Departure Bay ferry terminal in Naniamo …no, no I didn't bring it over this way. You see, my son Jeremy has been boarding with my brother-in-law at North Vancouver while attending U.B.C. and he acquired summer employment there at Rosco's Men's Wear last spring and thus he stayed there all summer. Now he had suggested to my brother-in-law, Hugo, in the spring, that he, Jeremy that is, being adept at carpentry, renovate Hugo's shed into a liveable accommodation, and since I possess a rather complete assemblage of carpentairial equipment, that he might borrow it for the summer. So I took it over last spring…yes I thought it was…pardon? …Oh my brother-in-law Hugo towed it down here into the line up for me…yes, it was wasn't it… why didn't I bring my vehicle to tow it home? Okay, okay, I'll admit I'm chintzy. I was born that way. And of course, it's too late to do anything about that now. I suppose that once this cloning technique is perfected that…but what really irks me is that a few years back you could be traveling across the country and if you saw a nice spot to camp you could simply pull over and camp. But now all roads are blocked off the highways and posted with signs, 'no trespassing', 'keep out', 'stay off', 'can't use,' 'it's mine'. I mean, people are as possessive with their personal effects as children with their toys. Now take this Ferry of yours, why don't you people permit animal towed conveyances on board?…In that case, supply shovels, for goodness sakes…and as for myself, *I'm* perfectly capable of using a washroom. I beg your pardon?… why of course…Why thank you, that's very helpful." The teacher hands the phone back to the girl.

"What did he say?" she asks.

"Wait until someone comes along with a hitch and ask for a tow to the other side," the teacher says, opening his frayed wallet. "So my fare will be one passenger plus the extra length for the trailer."

"Why didn't *I* think of that?" the girl asks herself, as she picks up the measuring stick and leaves the booth.

"Ah yes, experience is indeed an excellent teacher," the teacher says. "Why someday you *too* might become a 'superior'." He turns away from the toll girl to place his credit card on the sill of the booth but it slips from his fingers. He bends to pick it up. There is a moment of indecision, as the toll girl turns with stick in hand to see the polyester drawn taut across his butt. Wisely, she returns to the booth, taps out a ticket and pokes *it* at him.

The traveler's cheer and return to their vehicles and the traffic begin filing past the tollbooth. The teacher stands to one side with his trailer as he checks each car for hitches. When the newly weds pull up to the tollbooth, he notices the hitch on the rear of their Corsica. As the bridegroom is paying their fare, the teacher approaches the passenger side and asks the bride, "Could I have a tow."

"Oh, I'm terribly sorry," she replies. "But we don't smoke the stuff."

"No, no, no. A tow. I need someone to tow my trailer onto the ferry and off on the other side. My wife is waiting there with our vehicle."

"Oh so, you're married too. We just did it today…like the marriage thing?"

"That's nice. Now what about towing my trailer?"

"Oh, sure, sure, go right ahead. We're on our honeymoon, you see."

The teacher nods. "When your husband finishes paying his fare, please ask him to pull over here and I'll hook-up."

"Oh sure," she says. "You see, we just got married this afternoon and we are on our way to the Flopping Flounder Inn By the Sea to get our honeymoon going. I'm terribly excited about it and everything. You see, it's my first time…like the honeymooning thing? I'm terribly excited about it and everything." Then turning to her husband, she says, "Pull over here for a sec, dear."

Without questioning his newly attained wife motives, he does this. Quickly the teacher hooks up his trailer and jumps in the back seat.

"Why is there a man in our back seat?" the bridegroom seems anxious to know.

"Oh, I offered him a tow…just onto the ferry and off on the other side. He's married too. His wife is waiting for him over there. Isn't that nice of her? Isn't marriage marvellous, honey-bun?"

The groom glances at his brand new wife. "I certainly hope so."

The teacher rests a hand on the back of the front seat and leans forward. "I can't thank you two enough. You see, I was in somewhat of a predicament there with my trailer. You know they wouldn't let me pull it onto the ferry myself."

"Really!" the bridegroom exclaims. "Ah, sweetie, we have a problem here."

"We do?"

"Yes, we can't give him a tow, love. We have no hitch."

The bride turns to the teacher. "I'm terribly sorry but we can't give you a tow. We have no hitch."

"You must have a hitch. I've already hooked my trailer up."

The bride turns back to her husband. "But we must have a hitch, honey bunch. He already hooked his trailer up."

"Then we either have a hitch or we have a crazy man in our back seat."

The bride glances over her shoulder, then whispers to her newly attained husband, "Are you sure we don't have a hitch?"

"At this point in time, I'm not sure about anything," he says. Then glancing at the teacher in the rear view mirror, he leans to whisper something in his wife's ear. She turns to the teacher and says, "He was hoping to get a little…mmm…" Her words are interrupted by her husband's hand. "…on the ferry but he can wait until we…mmm."

"Never mind," the groom says, pulling the Corsica into the flow of ferry traffic.

"Do you travel this way often?" the bridegroom asks, as they bounce over the ramp onto the ferry and follow the signalman's waving hand.

"No, it's the first time," the teacher says.

"Ours too," the bride says. "Like the honeymooning thing?"

Moments later, the traffic is parked on board the ferry and the three are standing beside the Corsica.

"You are now traveling on B.C ferries. Do not remain on the car deck during your voyage but come up to the passenger deck and enjoy our facilities. The news-stand is…"

"Oh, isn't this exciting? We must go up stairs," the wife says. "I'm terribly excited and everything." Then turning to the teacher, she adds, "It's my first time on a ferry. I'm from Spuzzum, you see."

"I see."

"What will *you* do," the husband asks the teacher.

"Me? Do? Oh, just sit in your vehicle, I suppose."

"He was hoping to get a little…mmm…" the wife says.

When the groom removes his hand, he says, "Wouldn't you rather go upstairs and have something to eat?"

"Oh no. I never eat on the ferries. I think the prices are far out of line. I've brought an egg sandwich I made at my brother-in-law's place. Besides I have to stay and watch my belongings."

The husband scratches the back of his neck and tells his shoe. "Well, I don't actually know you that…ah…well, you know, to leave you…ah here…"

"I see," says the teacher. "You're afraid I might take something of yours?"

"Well…"

"Oh no," the wife says. "You seem like a terribly nice man. Besides, how could you run off with our car; I mean where would you hide it, eh?" She laughs, it's very much like one of those car alarms you often hear, shrill and never shut off soon enough.

"You are too kind," the teacher says, as the couple walks toward the stairs hand in hand.

Approximately an hours and thirty five minutes later, but slightly behind schedule due to a unavoidable delay at Horseshoe Bay, the Corsica pulls out of the steady stream of ferry traffic at Departure Bay to let the teacher unhook his trailer.

"I can't thank you two enough for the hitch," he says, after releasing his trailer. "And *do* have a pleasant honeymoon."

"We'll do our best," the two chant in unison.

The bride sticks her head out of the car window. "I just thought of a joke and it's terribly funny. We got hitched today and so did you, ha, ha, ha. Now isn't that terribly funny?"

The teacher nods, and as he watches the Corsica pull away, he agrees that it *was* terribly funny and that the couple were terribly nice and so was the toll girl and the crowd and that everyone has been so terribly nice on this terribly nice day. And as he saunters across the parking lot pulling his trailer, a poem that he has often taught in school comes to mind:

'Oh I *must* go down to the sea again,

To the wonderful sea and the sky,

And all I ask is...'

Across The River

"So what are you going to do this summer to earn enough to get you through another year?" This is what Nicole asks, Cody as they sit in Coffee Nook in the Crescent Valley Mall sipping coffee and spreading cream cheese on their bagels.

"There's no work for me around Crescent Valley but I have a cousin who lives in Prince George and he says I can get work down the line towards McBride at an isolated sawmill camp where his brother works. He's a mill-wright there and can get me work. The pay is good and, because of isolation, you get free room and board. They have a cookhouse and bunkhouses for workers. I would be able to save everything I earn and come back here next year with a payload. Sound's too good to be true, eh?"

"If it sounds too good to be true it probably is."

"Is what, 'true', or 'too good to be true'?"

"Pardon me?"

"Isn't the logical way of saying that expression; 'If it sounds too good to be true it probably isn't? Like 'isn't true?"

"For gosh sakes, Cody, what are you getting at?"

"Think about it."

"No you think about it, stuck in a place like that for four months with nothing to do but sit around with a bunch of uneducated guys…maybe read. You couldn't stand that."

Cody waves a dispelling hand. "Apparently you can go fishing in the rivers and the creeks, hunt ptarmigan, there's wild raspberries and strawberries."

"Oh sure, I can see you out by yourself in the wilderness picking berries. You don't own a gun and would be scared to use it if you did."

"Well it sounds like fun to me, something completely different from the routine town life we're used to."

"That I like," Nicole says. "Remember far away fields look green."

"If they look green they probably are."

"Oh Cody, where not going to argue another old adage."

"Okay, but you know how hard it is to get any kind of employment in this town so damn it, Nicole, I have to go for it."

"And where does that leave me?"

"You could come up to Prince George and I could run up there for a weekend with you once in a while."

"But think of the expense." Nicole gazes thoughtfully at Cody. "We're in love with each other. I don't know if I can handle this."

"We have to make some sacrifices if we are to get ahead."

"Get ahead of what?"

"You're used to a life where you can afford to get the things you want and go the places you want. When we get married, we'll want that kind of life, therefore I have to go to where I can earn enough money to get my education."

Nicole looks at Cody tearfully. "I'll be lonesome, Cody."

"And so will I but…"

They finish their snack quietly, Cody stealing glances of guilt. Nicole stealing glances of loss.

"It'll be fine, honey, the time will go fast and I'll be into my final year. That's what we've wanted all along, right?"

"Sure it is, but what a price to pay."

"We're spoiled. A lot of married couples have endured a lot more."

It's a week later that Cody is on the CNR heading up to McBride. Once the train leaves the town there's nothing much to see except wilderness. Something Cody's not at all familiar with. The click-clack of the wheels on the tracks meld with drowsy dip and rise of the telephone lines adding to the boredom that's invading Cody's being. *Maybe, Nicole was right; maybe, it'll be too much for me to endure. Oh sure, the beauties there: mountains rising high on either side of the rails that follow the big river's muddy path.*

The conductor walks through the passenger cars. "Next stop Sawmill Creek." The train stops and Cody steps down onto the plank platform in front of a small store and post office. A gray sign reads 'Sawmill Creek', its letters barely visible now from the elements. The proprietor of the store, obviously postmaster as well, trundles a dolly carrying the outgoing mailbag and parcels over to the freight car to exchange them with the incoming.

As the train pulls away, Cody stands surveying his new location of life. The warmth of the summer afternoon spreads a somnolent haze across the intervale. Beyond the railroad tracks and beyond the muddy river's far shore, the mountain's forested slopes rise, their peaks teased by a few wisps of clouds. Asbestos seeps from the ties, its pungency rising on the heat waves. Beyond the store lie the bunkhouses; a line of rectangle boxes; clapboard sides weather-grayed; tar papered roofs held down by strips of mill-slash. The cookhouse stands beyond of similar materials and workmanship but twice as wide. Smoke curls from a stack where the kitchen's situated and out back is a huge pile of split birch. A few private residence are scattered around; he suspects for families. They're not much compared with the city houses he's used to; they're those typical square cottage roof efforts seen in old mining camps.

As Cody's about to walk across the train-stop platform to the store, a figure catches the corner of his eye. The person's wearing leather pants scarred with scrapes and river mud, grease and dirt. The long knotted tangles of hair hanging well below her old felt hat, leads Cody to suspect that this person is female. A large hunting knife's buried in a sheath on a broad leather belt. Above she wears a leather jacket with the marks of her life imbedded in it. These clothes all appear to be hand made. Her features show signs of river mud and weathered tan. She's carrying an old trappers backpack. Looks heavy for a woman, but even though she's not much taller than Cody's six feet, she strides effortlessly up the grade and onto the platform toward the store entrance. She stops suddenly in her tracks; as a cougar might while stalking prey; is he easy prey? Or a deer might when startled by a snapped twig; no twig snapped: or did it? Standing motionless; slowly she turns; rivets a stealthy stare on Cody's eyes. He can see now that she's not at all old; not even middle aged. No telling if she's homely or not; in her attire and weather scared features. Slowly turning away, she walks on into the store. Cody follows in on a whiff, certainly no brand of a popular perfume.

The interior of the store reminds him of the old general stores you see on museum sites, like Barkerville or Dawson City, tall shelves with canned goods, large sacks of flour and sugar; grubstake supplies for hunters, trappers and prospectors. There's a row of stools along a short counter with a coffee percolator. A sign above it reads, 'Free coffee for customers'. Cody slides onto one of the stools and pours himself a coffee.

The woman's at the counter where the proprietor buys pelts. She lifts a stack of a dozen or so pelts out of her backpack and sets them on the counter. As the man leafs through the pelts, the two are silent. He clatters his cash register and takes out a couple of hundred dollar bills and hands them to her. She shakes her head, raising three fingers "Three," she says in a voice as soft as velvet that one wouldn't think came from this creature.

He just shakes his head.

"Then I'll keep," she says and goes to slip them back in her pack.

"No, no, hold on there, I'll give you three hundred."

He does and she frowns at him. Then she hands him a slip of paper. "I want these."

The whole time, the storekeeper is rounding up these groceries, this wild woman steals glances at Cody. This can be expected because Cody is a good-looking guy in his mid-twenties and has a face that likes to smile. She pays for her groceries and puts them in her backpack. "Mail?'

"Yes." He goes into his post office nook and brings out two packages. She glances at the addresses on them and tosses them into her backpack.

"Gas," she says, and turns to leave but when she reaches the door and lays a hand on the knob, she turns and looks at Cody. He smiles. She fixes a stare at him that feels like two sharp knives are driven half way through his scull. The door opens; she's gone.

Cody looks over at the proprietor. "If looks could kill, eh?" Then he gets to his feet and walks over to the counter. "Hi, I'm Cody Billings, come to work here for the summer." He extends a hand.

"Hi fella, Jim Johnson."

They shake.

"That's an odd one, eh?" Cody says. "Where's she from?"

"Oh, that's Rachel Small. She lives in that little house across the river: sad thing though. When she was ten, her parents drowned trying to cross the river on the early ice. Fell through: ten years old she was; pulled them out but it was too late; buried them herself, yes sir she did, right in front of her house: she marked graves with wooden crosses. It was a sad sight to see. People tried to get her to come over here. They offered to take her in; in fact they brought her forcibly at first. Wouldn't stay. Thought she'd die over there on her own; cold winters. Only ten years old, you see. Yes sir, you and I have no idea: the heartache, eh? Pluck? Geez man, I'll say she's got pluck, she survived trapping, hunting and homesteading all by herself, but her tragic loss and no one else who mattered to her, eh? Turned her wild, a damned shame. Oh she accepts me because she's known me since she was just a little girl but when I don't give her what she wants for her furs, I see that wild look in her eyes and give her what she wants.

"But the mail you gave her, what was it all about?"

"You see, when this happened, the schoolteacher here sent away for correspondence courses for her schooling. When they came in the mail, I made sure Rachel got them. She would send stuff back and have stuff returned to her so I figured she must have been doing them. And she orders books too, something to keep her busy in her loneliness, I guess."

"Sounds to me like there's a lot of normal woman under her; what you call wildness."

"Yeah, I'd agree with you there, but she can become violent if she feels threatened; like one of those wild animals in those mountains: her only friends."

"So she must know something about the world she's never seen."

"Oh yes, and she's smart. That's not the problem. What I think, now I'm no psychologist, but I think she's afraid to make friends for fear of losing them like she did her parents."

Cody nods. "I think you're right about that but living in isolation will cause paranoia too."

"You sound a hell of a lot like a psychologist."

"That's what I'm studying at university." Cody picks up a chocolate bar off a rack of assorted candies and lays it on the counter. "I had free coffee so I guess I got to buy something…but you know Jim, that little girl she once was has got to be hidden somewhere inside her."

"You better not try to find her, fella, one of the young mill guys went over there to her place, to 'you know what', get a little friendly, eh? He barely made it back across the river alive. He had a back eye and scratched face had to go to Prince hospital, cracked ribs and broken arm."

"Wow, she must have taken after him with a club."

"He said she never used any weapon, it should have been a fair fight, as fair as a fight between and unarmed woman and an unarmed man could be, eh?"

"That huge hunting knife, does she always wear it?"

"Whenever, I see her. But she rarely comes over accept to the store. Oh, I've seen her use it once when a new mill crew guy made some wisecrack at her. She was just leaving the store and he was standing just outside the door. He made the remark as she went past and she said nothing but when she got off the platform, and she was, oh I'd say about forty feet away, she spun around as quick as a cat and threw that knife. It nicked his ear and stuck in the front of the store. The guy stood frozen with shock."

"Next time I'll put it through your skull," she said pulling the knife from the wall.

Cody shakes his head. "Oh my God."

"Just so you know what you're up against, Cody, just so you know."

Cody frowns on that thought and paces around for several minutes before asking. "So where do I find the mill office?"

"You see that little shack beside those sidetracked boxcars?"

"Yes."

"That's it."

On his way to the office he passes this woman walking up from the river with a jerry can in each hand.

"Hi, Rachel," he says, with a smile as they pass. "Nice to meet you."

She glances at him furtively remaining silent.

In the office he mentions his cousins name and gets signed up for employment.

At first you will be getting jobs to do when others don't show up. It happens a lot especially early in the week after the boys have gone to Prince for the weekend. But we'll keep you busy, piling lumber, shovelling sawdust out from underneath the trimmer and edger. You know what they are?"

"No."

"Are you in good shape?"

"Sure, lots of athletics at university."

"Well, some of these jobs are muscle work all day, but you'll get toughened up. This slip shows your bunkhouse number and bunk."

"Thanks."

When Cody comes out of the office, this wild woman walks by on her way back down toward the river carrying two jerry cans obviously full of gas.

As she draws abreast of him, Cory says, "Would you like me to help you?"

There's a quick glance and a slight headshake as she trudges by.

Cody says, "Good bye for now, Rachel, looking forward to seeing you again."

There's no reply, no reaction and really no effort as she lifts the loaded jerry cans into her riverboat at the boat landing.

Cody leans against a boxcar. Wow, she's strong.

This woman gets into her boat, gives one yank on the rope and the motor purrs. She sits down and scoots her riverboat across the river. She points the bow at an angle slightly up stream so the rushing current will send her straight across. The Fraser River's wide here, but Cody can still clearly see her tie up on the small wharf by her house, and with his good eye sight even some small detail is visible.

Gosh, what a lonely existence. And Nicole thought I'd be lonesome living over here on this side. Maybe I will; but nothing compared with what that woman has endured.

Cody watches her pause to look back across the river to where he stands. He waves. For a minute or so, she watches Cody. Then she begins packing things from the boat up the bank to her house. She stops at the door to look his way then goes in. He turns and carries his suitcase up to the bunkhouse he was designated. It's empty now, because everyone's working. Beds are lined up along either side. There's a line of coat hooks on the wall between the beds and a small roughly constructed bedside desk. There's no dresser for clothes. They stay in the suitcase to be slid under the bed.

Cody lies down on the bed for it's only three and falls asleep. The five o'clock steam whistle blows from the mill awakening Cody. By the time he gets to his feet and opens the bunkhouse door, the mill workers stream out of the mill like ants from a disturbed anthill. They head for the cookhouse on the rush. Cody's last to enter. He stands and watches. Anything vaguely con-nected with manners have obviously been abandoned from their curriculum, as they stand reaching, grabbing before the next guy gets something they don't. Why? There's plenty of food and quality food too. It's necessary if they want a good hard working crew in camp. Once they have all offerings within reach, they sit and gorge themselves. It reminds Cody of pigs at a trough.

His cousin, Sam, the millwright sees him standing there and motions him over.

"You'll get only scraps to eat unless you pitch in like these buggers are. They're animals, not men. You sit here beside me until they get used to you." Sam stands and fills a plate for Cody and places it in front of him.

"Thanks, Sam."

" I seen you trying to get friendly with that wild woman, better not. They say she was attacked by a cougar and killed it with a hunting knife. She got scratched up a lot but she won. You know how fast and strong a house cat is, well you just blow that cat up ten or twenty sizes bigger and you can imagine fighting it off. The whole damned crew is scared of her. Jim, the storekeeper's okay with her because he knew her and her parents before they drowned. As long as he gives her what she wants for her furs, she's okay with him. But she could take them to Prince and get twice as much but I guess she doesn't know that. She never leaves here. Twice a month on payday, the crew goes to Prince George on the Friday evening local train. They get pissed and screwed all weekend and come back broke and do it all over again next payday."

"Hookers?"

"Oh sure, they're waiting like leaches to steal their money. I suppose the buggers get their money's worth and that's what they live for. They'll have a few squirrels in your bed when you go to get in it but pretend you didn't know and let them think they pulled one over on you. Your socks will be tied together in the morning. You're too clean cut for there liking. Hope you can defend yourself. You look pretty husky but there are a few who gang up; don't care about fair play."

"Not a problem, four years of boxing training and tournament competition at UBC. I've sparred with pros too."

"It should help but they can fight dirty too."

"I don't scare easily."

"Being sacred isn't the problem. I've seen some poor innocent buggers get beat pretty bad."

After supper Cody goes to the cook and asks if he can make a couple of turkey sandwiches for himself.

"Hey Bud, no problem, there's always lots of leftovers that get thrown to the dogs if no one wants them."

"Thanks man, you're okay." With the sandwiches, in a paper bag, Cody wanders back to the shore of the river. He sits down on a log looking across and nibbles on a sandwich. How could he be hungry after that big supper? He isn't: so why the sandwiches? He doesn't sit long before he sees her. Grizzly Woman? No, Rachel come out and sit on the wharf looking over at him. He waves but she doesn't wave back. He eats his sandwich although it's a struggle. Then he lifts the other sandwiches out of the bag and holds them so she can see. Then he places them in the paper bag and sets it on a post by the boat landing and drops the chocolate bar in, then waves to her and walks away. He doesn't go far; hides behind some shrubbery. He figured her right; she steps into her riverboat and scoots over. Leaving the motor chugging, she hurries up to the post, gets the bag and leaves in a hurry. But Cody sensed that she knew where he was hiding; call it wilderness vigilance: a means of surviving. Cody sits on the log and gazes across the river. Back on her wharf, she sits and eats her gift: the sandwiches then the chocolate bar. He waves. No response. He leaves. "Poor little girl locked inside her can't get out, hopefully all she needs is a friend."

Back in the bunkhouse, several guys are playing poker. They glance up as Cody enters but say nothing. Then a big burly bugger lying back in his bunk says, "Where the hell are you from, pretty boy?"

"Crescent Valley."

"Crescent Valley, hear that Butch? Well ain't that cute. What do you do?"

"I'm a university student trying to earn enough money for next term."

"Gee-zuz-kee-rist, I hate you educated buggers." He nods to the guy in the next bunk "Come on Butch and Rod, let's take this candy-assed city slicker outside and knock some of the fucking education out of him."

One of the guys playing poker says, "Lay off the kid, Hank, let him get his feet wet first."

"The hell I will, hey, kid are you too chicken to step outside with us?"

Cody opens the door. "So you got to gang up, do you? Too cowardly to fight one at a time." Cody steps outside. He expected the challenge he gave them would mean only one at a time would attack. He was wrong. Three guys come out of the bunkhouse. They hate educated people that much? I guess.

As the three try to circle Cody to attack from three sides, they hear a sharp yell. "One at a time."

All four turn to look; it's Grizzly Woman standing back about fourty feet, fists on hips; hunting knife clearly visible at her belt. Again she yells, "Only one at a time."

Three attackers look at each other, then Hank nods. He steps up first. He takes a lunge at Cody who snaps his head back with three vicious left jabs. Hank steps back to stare, glances over at Grizzly Woman, then he moves in and throws a straight right. Cody catches it in his right hand and throws a left hook over top that lands flush on the jaw and down goes Hank.

"Next," Grizzly Woman yells.

Butch moves in on Cody. By this time the whole mill crew, the cooks and flunkies are all standing in front of the bunkhouses watching. Even the mill owner and foreman are out watching with their wives and children: even the schoolteacher. Butch moves in for the kill but runs into a fast flurry of punches driving him back twenty feet. Then Cody's left hook puts Butch flat on his back.

The crowd cheers.

Now it's Rod's turn. He doesn't seem so anxious now.

"Next," she yells.

Rod moves up and squares off. Cody decides to make this one a convincing job, one to send a message to the others. He steps in quickly with four lightning fast head-snapping jabs that send blood splashes in the air. A right to the bottom of Rod's rib cage doubles him up. As he tries to catch his breath, Cody steps in with a right uppercut straightens him for a left hook and he's down and out.

"Next." She yells again.

"I think that's all the takers, Grizz," one of the crew yells. "I don't think anyone else will bother your boy friend for the whole summer. If they try ganging up on him I'm sure you'll be back."

The crowd cheers raucously as the three lugs crawl up out of the dirt.

Cody looks at Rachel, who's watching the three bullies try to stand up. "Thanks, Rachel, that was very sweet of you to help me."

It's the word 'sweet' that snaps Rachel's eyes onto Cody's. It also sends a few glances from others at Cody then Grizzly. It's as if they can't see where Cody sees any sweetness. Of course, he doesn't really, but he knows it's there. Her gaze remains fixed on him until most of the crowd has dispersed, then without a word, she walks down to her boat, gets in and scoots across the river.

An older mill worker steps over and shakes Cody's hand. "Well, you young buck, you can sure handle your dukes, and you sure must have a way with the ladies to get *her* on your side. She would have cleaned up on the whole works of us if you'd asked her to."

As things turned out, there were no squirrels in his bed that night, whether Grizzly Woman had sneaked in and taken them out or the mill boys were afraid to put them there, it's hard to say. Cody lies on his bed and writes a letter to Nicole; just a brief note for he doesn't have much to say to her; just a brief mention of the fight but nothing about the, so called, wild woman helping him or his kindness toward her.

Due to yesterday's nap, last night's fracas and the loud snoring, Cody can't sleep. It's beginning to get light so he slips out of bed quietly and walks down to the river. He sits where he can watch the light blue of the pre-morning sunrise silhouette the eastern mountain range; its gradual transformation of magenta hues to ochre until a spark ignites the mountain's fringe. Then its rays stream across the river alighting a window of her cottage. Its reflection catches the corner of Cody's eye turning his attention toward her sitting on her wharf and sipping from a cup and watching him.

This mystery woman, this Grizzly woman, as they call her, she came across the river to help me. She must have known ahead of time what they'd try to do to me. And why was she so concerned for me? The turkey sandwiches and bar; an act of friendship. And how did she know I'd be able to handle one at a time? Maybe, she didn't; maybe she wanted to see what kind of a man I was.

He waves. No response. The two sit and look at each other, two complete strangers. Both lonely: one far from home; the other where her home has always been but empty of love, of caring for the last fifteen years. He sheds a tear for his loneliness and a tear for hers. It isn't until the cookhouse gong shatters the silence that Cody gets to his feet. He waves again but no response.

"You'll do the green chain," George Randle, the foreman, lets him know. "I'll go down and show you the ropes."

The mill whistles sounds and the wheels of production begin turning. The trimmer saws sing slicing through the 2X4 ends just before they slide down onto the green chain and move toward him.

"They have to be piled on the correct piles according to their length. See those chains hanging down there, they show you the length but you'll get to know just by looking at them after while: furthest eighteen feet, next closest sixteen feet and so on by two foot lengths. These numbers on the walkway here show the piles by length on which they go. When these are so high you can't pile anymore here, another series of piles can be started further down the green chain. Look about forty feet down there; see the numbers on the walk; that's where they go. Then you go down there and pile and a jitney will take these away to be piled in boxcars. The lumber comes fast at times and there's no rest until coffee break at ten. You better be in good shape. Go to it lady killer."

George laughs and slaps Cody on the back. Cody laughs too.

Things go okay for Cody but the lumber comes fast and about nine thirty he's ready for a rest but it's another half hour until coffee break. They must have gotten into some bigger logs because the green chains more heavily loaded with 2X4's, 2X6's and 2X8's. They're all different lengths and so the choice of piles becomes much more complex. Cody can't keep up but he pulls them off and piles them as fast as he can. Of course, some are getting by him but what can he do? After a while they get into smaller logs and things slow down a little but what about all those boards he missed. He turns around expecting to see a crisscrossed mess of lumber sky high at the end of the green chain but no; Rachel's down where the other piles are to go, she's sliding boards off the green chain fast onto the correct piles. She's much faster and stronger than he is. She doesn't look his way and he doesn't have time to look at her as the lumber keeps coming. As he resumes his work, he lets some go by so he can rest a bit and see what she'll do. He can hear her sliding them into their piles quickly and effortlessly.

What would I have done if she hadn't come along?

The ten o'clock whistles sounds and he turns but she's gone. He sits down and opens his thermos and pours a coffee. The trimmer-man walks down the steps over to Cody. He offers his hand. "Hi, fella, I'm John Tran."

"I'm Cody Billings. This damned lumber comes down pretty fast at times."

"Yeah, the jobs on the different saws, like the trimmer here takes more know-how but are easier. This is the toughest job in the mill. That's why they have to keep getting new guys."

"Well, they *could* put two guys on the chain."

"Costs more money. Hell, man, what are you complaining about, you got a helper. I don't know what you got going for you, Billings, but no ones ever had that effect on that wild woman."

"Maybe, she isn't really wild, John, maybe there's a real tender woman under that dirt. I aim to find out."

John roars with laughter. "Well, if you can tame her all the more power to you but…" He just shakes his head. "You don't know her like we do. Wild? Oh she's wild all right, you'll find out; she's like one of those lone wolves up in those mountains, she's lived alone in the wild too long, man, too long. She'll tear you apart if you get too close. We've seen it, yeah man, we've all seen it. Why do you think those three bullies wouldn't attack you at the same time? Hell, that should tell you. Better watch your step, man, watch your step." John smiles at Cody's naivety and turns as the whistle sounds.

And so the day is only quarter over and Cody's muscles are tired and sore. *I don't know how I'm going to make it through the day.* He gets to his feet sets his thermos where it won't get broken and gets ready to get back to work, but just before the trimmer saws whine he hears steps further down the green chain. He turns and she's sitting on the end of a pile of 2X6's. She glances at him furtively then away. She's shucked her heavy clothing and is wearing blue jeans and a sleeveless t-shirt. She's nicely built and although still dirty and vigilant, she looks much more like a woman. Her muscular arms bare the scars of the cougar's claws and the large shoulder muscle near her neck bares the imprints of the cougar's fangs; the cougar almost had her.

"Thanks Rachel, I wouldn't have survived the morning if you hadn't helped me."

She's had to survive wild animals, starvation, sadness, all alone.

She steals a quick glance then looks at her hands and says nothing. She helps Cody the rest of the morning but when the dinner-whistle sounds she disappears again. As Cody approaches the cookhouse, he can hear the men's loud voices and laughter within. But as he opens the door, a hush falls over the crew like a soft flannel blanket. Then as Cody fills his plate from the food table and sits down beside Sam, a soft drone of muttering moves about and heads turn and mouths whisper.

"I hear you had a helper this morning, Cody," Sam says.

Cody laughs. "It appears everyone's heard that."

"They're amazed, so am I. They've seen her in action."

"Meaning she's a wild animal that's likely to kill me if I get too close, right?"

"Yes sir, exactly."

"And what do you think Sam?"

"Well Cody, I'll say this much, you have an effect on her no one else ever has, but you know, even a tamed wild animal can turn on you."

"But," Cody says, "She was tame to begin with, that's where the difference lies."

When Cody returns to the green chain, a jitney is taking the last of the piles away. It'll be a bit easier piling until the late afternoon when they get high again. The sun has moved around and will be beating down on him all afternoon. As he turns back to the green chain, he sees a sweating canvass water-bag hanging from a spike just below the green chain and a straw sun hat lying on the walk below. Rachel's not in sight but he knows she brought these things to ease his day and he knows she'll be back to help. And of course, he's right. As soon as the whistle blows and the wheels start turning, he hears her footsteps but the lumbers coming now so he doesn't have time to look her way.

The second and third weeks unfold in much the same manner. But on the evening of the last day of the third week, when he puts bagged sandwich on the post, he decides not to hide. As usual, she gets into her boat and runs across. Seeing him still sitting there, she stays in her boat, gazing at him, her motor softly purring. Then she steps onto the wharf and walks warily up to the post. As she picks up the bag, she smiles at Cody.

"Hi, Rachel, you're a really nice girl. I like you, do you like me?"

"Yes," she says and like a startled cat scurries back to leap into her boat and speed away. Back at her home, she sits on the wharf and eats while they watch each other.

The fourth week continues this way but for a few changes. She's sitting on a lumber pile down at her end of the green chain when Cody arrives Monday morning. There's a lunch pail for him where he works. She's clean in both clothes and skin and for the first time, he can see that she's no beauty but she has fine feminine features that want to be friendly. As usual, she works hard helping him and when the wheels stop for coffee and lunch breaks, she stays.

"You look really nice today, Rachel, you know, the way you're dressed."

Looking down at the board walkway, Rachel says, "You look nice too, Cody."

It's Friday evening and being payday and the crew has caught the 'local' for Prince George. Upon finishing his supper at the cookhouse, Cody goes to the store to check for mail but there's been no reply from his note to Nicole. He goes to the river and sits looking over at her cottage. She's not in sight. After wandering around camp kicking rocks at the gnawing ache of loneliness, he saunters back to the river; looking across, there's no Rachel in slight.

I may as well go to the bunkhouse and turn in for the night.

The morning sun breaks through the bunkhouse window tracing a path across Cody's features awakening him. He's rested and his muscles seem to be getting used to the work.

Some food and I'll go to the riverbank to read. Don't suppose I'll see Rachel though; she disappears somewhere on weekends.

As Cody reads, he looks up often to see if there's any life over at Rachel's cottage. By late morning, the sun has swung around the stand of cottonwoods that line the river and its hazy warmth puts him to sleep.

It's the purring of her riverboat that awakens Cody. Rachel ties her boat to the wharf pilling, slips a backpack on her back, lifts two jerry cans out and heads up the bank.

"Need some help?" Cody asks.

Without looking his way, she shakes her head and strides effortlessly up the bank toward the store. As soon as she enters, Cody gets to his feet and follows. She gives Cody a startled stare as he walks in the door. But when she sees him go to the coffee percolator and pour himself a coffee and slide onto one of the stools, that momentary vigilance fades away.

Hmm, she acted friendlier lately with her smiles but she's more vigilant this morning; maybe just typical womanly mood swings.

She turns her attention to Jim and they settle the fur trade.

When she looks back at Cody, he has poured another coffee and holds it toward her. "Like a fresh coffee, Rachel?"

She looks frightened at first. "I'll set it here for you, Rachel, you'll like it. It tastes real good." He sets the cup on the counter several feet away. She studies the situation for a minute or so then walks over, sets her backpack down at the foot of a stool further away. She must reach to get her coffee cup. At first she won't look his way but after a few sips she turns and gazes at him. He smiles at her. "It's a nice morning isn't it?"

She nods and smiles. They just sit and gaze at each other. "It's been so sweet of you to help me like you have, Rachel. I'm not used to such hard work. If I get some sandwiches from the cookhouse, would you sit on the riverbank with me so we can have lunch together? It's okay if you don't want to but what do you think?"

Rachel looks away and her shoulders cringe a little. "I...I...I'd like to." She looks down and bites her lip.

"It's okay, Rachel, I care, remember that Rachel, I care."

She nods, steps off the stool, picks up her backpack and is out the door.

"My God fella, you're reaching her heart. No one else ever has been able to come close to doing that. But you know, if she comes around to normal, you can never leave her or she'll die."

"Yeah, Jim, I know that, but someone's got to save her."

"It's a big sacrifice to give your life for another's."

"You know, Jim, there's something quite lovable about her."

Jim chuckles. "It sound's like she's starting to get to *you*, Cody."

Cody goes back to the river where he's left his book. Her boats back on the other side. The sun is now shinning directly against the riverbank filling Cody with warmth that sooths him into slumber. The cookhouse gong awakens him.

I forgot to make sandwiches.

As he sits up and wipes sleep from his eyes, he sees her there. She's sitting in her boat. Then he almost bumps into a bucket sitting beside him.

She's been close to me, as close as she's ever been.

The bucket's full of food: four small drumsticks, and several eggs, broccoli heads, radishes and green onions.

All this food wasn't meant for just me. She wants to eat with me. He looks down at her in the boat. "Hi Rachel, you can come up and sit and eat lunch with me if you want to."

She doesn't move.

He knows what he has to say; he doesn't really want to but he must. "Don't be afraid Rachel, I love you."

Slowly she moves up the bank and sits about six feet away from him with the bucket in between. Cody hands the bucket her way so she can reach in. Her hand reaches; shaking; it takes out the other drumstick.

"Thanks," she says in a trembling voice.

"Why won't you sit closer to me, you like me, don't you?"

She looks at the ground and nods.

"Do you love me?"

She nods.

"Rachel, look at me and tell me that you love me."

"I'm afraid to."

"Why?'

"I'm afraid you'll leave me like they did." Her whole body trembles and she bursts into sobs.

There goes her defence mechanism. Now what the hell do I do?

Cody moves the bucket and slides over to her. He wraps his arms around her and holds her tight. "I'll never leave you Rachel, I love you too much. Cry it all out so you'll never be sad and lonely again."

She clings to him as he holds her soothingly, gently rocking her, for now she's as dependent on his nurturing as an infant. They remain like this for a long time. Then Cody holds her back to see her face. "Rachel, smile at me."

She smiles.

"That's what you have to practise doing. Smiling at me and telling me that you love me because that's what I'm going to be doing to you." He smiles. "I love you Rachel. Do you love me?"

She starts to nod.

"No Rachel, look at me and smile and say it."

She lifts her eyes to him and smiles. "I love you Cody. Please don't ever…" She bites back tears. "… leave me."

"I won't Rachel; never. Now I want us to go over to your house. I want you to know what it's like to be a woman loved by a man."

"I'm afraid to."

"I'm afraid too, Rachel, so let's go and be afraid together, okay?"

"Okay."

They get in her boat and cross the river.

Cody's cousin, Sam has been watching them from behind some bushes. As they reach the far shore, he turns and walks over to the store. "Well, Jim, guess what?'

"What?"

"Cody just left with Rachel in her boat for her house."

"Yeah, he was getting to her heart this morning. She sat down and had a couple of sips of coffee at the coffee bar with him and he invited her to have lunch with him on the riverbank. Do you think Cody can handle her, Sam?"

"I didn't realize how strong mined he is. Of course, I seen him a lot as a kid but how he stood up to those guys in the fight and how he treated Rachel like a normal woman; well it really surprised me. I think he can handle her, I really do."

"Well, he's got a big problem because some woman called Nicole, phoned and said she was in Prince and to tell him to come and spend the night with her."

"Oh my God, that's his fiancé. Did she leave a number?"

"Yeah."

"All we can do is wait until Cody comes back across the river."

"What if he doesn't?"

"Who said life's dull in a sawmill camp?"

The phone rings. Jim answers. "He's not here right now, Nicole. I'll let you talk to his cousin Sam, he's right here."

"Hi Nicole, you should have let him know you were coming…what's he up to? All I can say is you should go back to Crescent Valley and get on with your life…No, no, that would not be a good idea…why? Because a sawmill camp is no place for a woman…look Nicole, it would be easier on you and him if…oh shit she hung up and she's catching the 'local' for here. It gets in at five."

"Right."

The five o'clock 'local' stops and a pretty lady in a black dress and white shawl steps off with her suitcase. Sam's waiting there to meet her.

"Where is he?" she seems anxious to know.

"Damn you, Nicole, I warned you not to come. You've put yourself and Cody in a dangerous situation."

"Oh really, Samuel, what can possibly be dangerous in this hole in the wall. Tell me where that bastard is. He's with another woman, isn't he?"

"Yeah, Nicole he is, and she's capable of tearing both you and Cody apart and she'll do it if you push things."

"Don't be silly, Sam, she's a woman, at least that's what you said, correct?"

"Yeah, she's a woman, but not like any you've ever run across."

"Cody's quite capable of looking after himself. He can box. He told me about the fights he had."

"Did he tell you why they only attacked him one at a time?"

"No."

"Because she was standing there threatening the whole damned crew and they listened to her. Doesn't *that* tell you anything?"

"I don't know why, Samuel, but you're trying to scare me away from him."

"Let me tell you something Nicole, this woman saw her parents drown in that river when she was ten years old. She pulled them out but it was too late. She buried them in the front yard of that house you see across the river; all by her self, and has lived in that wilderness ever since trapping and hunting to survive. She's as strong and as quick as a wild cat. She was attacked by a cougar and killed it before it killed her. There's not a man in this camp who has the courage to stand up to her. Cody's taught her to accept him through kindness. He saw a lost woman and he did it to save her. Do you understand, Nicole? Cody's sacrificing his life to save a drowning woman. It's as simple as that."

"Does he love her more than me?"

"That's not the issue. Would you push a person who can't swim into that turbulent river?"

Nicole lowers her head. "I want to at least talk to him."

"Then get back on the next train to Prince and wait until he calls you. If you don't you could both end up dead; she's a living time bomb right now."

"I must see him. Is he over there?"

"I don't know where he is. Nicole, for cripes sakes, come to my house and wait."

She runs down to the riverbank and yells. "Cody, it's me Nicole."

Cody and Rachel have been lying on a grassy knoll beside her home. Rachel's eyes and ears are those of a cougar's. She jumps to her feet. "Who is that Cody, who is that woman?"

As Cody gets up, Nicole calls again. "It's me, Nicole, Cody."

"She's your woman. You lied to me, you lied to me."

Cody sees the violence in her eyes but he's not quick enough or strong enough. He feels the pain and the ground strike his back. And she's on him, fist raised to strike, but it hesitates.

Back across the river, Nicole says, "Oh my God, she'll kill him."

"That's what I've been trying to tell you."

Nicole yells at the top of her lungs. "Don't Rachel, don't hurt him, he's yours. Don't hurt him; he loves you, not me. Don't harm him, he's yours."

Rachel's raised fist hovers above his face. It has even before Rachel heard Nicole's plea. She could have stuck him ten times in that time but she didn't.

"You heard her, Rachel. I'm yours. You wouldn't harm the only person who loves you, who cares enough to give her up for you. Think about it Rachel, now smile and tell me that you love me like we practised. I love you Rachel, always."

Her arm goes limp and she collapses on Cody. "And I love you, Cody. Please don't leave me."

He hugs her tight. "Okay, sweetheart, you and I are going over to the other side and tell her I'm going to marry you and raise a family like you've dreamed. But over on that land past the sawmill where our children and us won't have to cross this damned river."

As Sam and Nicole watch the two distance figures get to their feet and into her boat, Sam says, "Well Nicole, you've done what Cody's done, given up someone you love to save another."

"She needs him to survive. I can survive without him. I won't be easy getting him out of my mind but there's been guys hounding me all summer to date me. I won't have any trouble finding another love."

"You got character as well as beauty, Nicole; you're okay, girlie, you're okay."

Rachel's boat pulls up to the wharf. She springs out like cat, spins the rope around the pilling and strides toward Nicole. Rachel's quick powerful movements and penetrating stare step Nicole back a few paces.

"Easy honey," Cody says, catching Rachel's hand as if to hold her back. Forget it. One vigorous snap of her arm sends Cody flying face first into the water. When Cody's head comes up, he says, "Easy Rachel, she told you I love you and not her. She's leaving on the next 'local'. Right, Nicole?"

By this time Nicole's moved well back and is standing behind Sam's shoulder. "Why, yes, yes, of course, he's yours Rachel, I don't want him... he's yours..."

Rachel stops. Her searing stare slowly softens and she looks at Cody standing chest deep in the water. Reaching down with one hand, she grabs his hand and lifts him up onto the wharf like a parent would lift a child.

Still behind Sam's shoulder, Nicole says, "My God, Rachel, you're strong; how did you get so strong?"

Rachel turns; and as she lifts her eyes to the forested mountains rising beyond her home, they sense her awe, respect yet sentiment for this wilderness that was both her friend and enemy for so long. She points. "The weak animals die out there."

"You were dying until Cody rescued you, Rachel," Nicole says.

Rachel turns and frowns at Nicole as if bewildered. "How?'

"Without human love, Rachel, the humanness of a person dies no matter where they live."

Rachel stares at Nicole for a second looks away and nods. As Cody's arm encircles her, the tears start to flow. "I...I know."

"Goodbye Nicole," Cody says, "And thanks for caring too."

Nicole looks at Cody, bites her lip, nods and walks away.

Free Fall

Protocol seems normal on this particular Friday morning in mid January at Crescent Valley High School: if normal means everything is falling into place. Ben Dent, senior physics and biology teacher, bursts through the front door whistling 'Zippety Do Da', to the swing of his grip. He turns as Miss Sprite, girl's Physical Education teacher, trots up the front steps. Ben holds the door open for her, as his grip sweeps a path of chivalry before her. Her bright red tights stretch taunt to her form in the wake of her red scarf.

"My but we're bright eyed and bushy tailed this morning," she says, stopping to stomp snow from her boots. "Did last nights snowfall brighten your world?"

"Oh yes," he chuckles. "Nothing can match the soft newness of a fresh snowfall."

"You might not feel that way if you had to shovel the high ridge the snow plough left in front of my driveway. It took me almost an hour to shovel through."

"I live in a condo complex. There's a maintenance man who does the shoveling."

"That's good, middle aged men are prone to heart attacks and shouldn't shovel snow."

Ben's grip slumps to his side as the door swings shut.

"Maybe that's what *I* need…a maintenance man…a young one."

A blast of chill strikes Ben, as Gus Fullmer, boy's Physical Education teacher, walks through the door kicking snow from his galoshes. "What say, Dent, *old boy*? Quite a night, eh? It was snowing heavy when I left my adult

Keith Field

fitness group last night at nine thirty. Must have continued through most of the night."

"Yes, it was snowing at one o'clock when I went to bed."

"Up pretty late for a school night, weren't you?"

"I suppose it would be considered late for *older* people. But I had a student who needed assistance, and you know me, always ready to help."

Gus chuckles. "To help, eh? He or she?"

"She…in physics."

Gus gives a snort. "Why am I not surprised?"

All the while, Ben's eyes have been fixed on Sprite's taut departure.

Gus shakes his head. "Really Ben, you should be married at your age. Now there's one for you. Mind you, Miss Sprite is twenty five…a little young for you…but if you joined my adult fitness group, you could reduce that middle-age decline considerably."

"You're as young as you feel."

The buzzer interrupts their conversation and sets the wheels of education in motion, sending Gus to the auditorium and Ben toward the staff room.

If there are any irregularities unfolding within this establishment of learning this bright morning, no one seems to be aware of it. The distant clatter of the maintenance men's shovels melds in minds with theorems, theories and metaphors. On stage in the auditorium, Gus is coaching the junior boys in weight lifting, while on the main floor, Miss Sprite is instructing the junior girls in gymnastics.

The snap of ceiling tile sends eyes aloft. Is last night's snowfall breaking through? Surely twenty-five centimeters of snow isn't enough to break those sturdy trusses that interlace the loft. But the ceiling tiles part and two students drop through clinging frantically to the edges of the hole. It's immediately apparent that they are of opposite gender. Miss Sprite's whistle shrieks. She spits it out.

"Quickly, quickly girls, pile the mats beneath them to break their fall. Pamela and Jennifer stop staring and grab that end. Sylvia and Daphne stop staring and grab the other end. Hustle now; they can't hang on for long."

When the mats are stacked three tier deep, Miss Sprite signals. "Now let's circle the mats in case they careen of the mat when they land. Okay, you two up there. You can drop now. The mats will break your fall."

42

In keeping with the law of 'free-falling-bodies', they strike the mats at the same time. Their bounce sends a wave of hushed 'Oh wows' around the mat's perimeter. The two are Brad Hanson, president of the Student Council and star basketball player and Madeline Murchison, vice-president of the Student Council and basketball cheerleader.

"Now girls! Allow them to pass through and find their clothing."

Somewhat reluctantly, they part, allowing the couple to sprint toward the stage. Pam nudges Jennifer. "So finally it's happened. Like I told Zack the other day, that thin plywood will break through someday."

"Yeah, really," Jennifer says, "I mean, like actually, they *could* have taken it easy, eh?"

"Oh sure, sure. Can you?"

Jennifer shrugs. Dropped barbells resound off the stag floor, as the couple climb onto the stage

"Stop staring boys," Gus says, as he stares at the couple ascending the ladder to the loft.

Miss Sprite seems unsure of what protocol is called for. She looks up at Mr. Fuller, who senses her plea. He shrugs. She shakes a disgusted frown at him, climbs onto the stage and yells from the bottom of the ladder. "Get your clothes on and get down here this instance, you two." She turns and glances at Gus and his class of boys, who are still gazing up at the opening into the loft where the two were last seen. "It might be an idea to resume your weight training class, Gus."

"Yes, yes, of course. Okay boys, shows over at your local strip-joint."

A few groans meld with a few chuckles as the clank of pumping iron resumes.

Miss Sprite turns to her class, who are leaning their elbows on the edge of the stage while craning their necks to see up the ladder.

"Shower girls, shower."

"Make it a cold one," a boy yells.

The school principal, Mr. Weedley, the school secretary, Miss. Plummer, and several teachers are sitting around the conference table drinking coffee when Miss Sprite bounds into the staff room. "Mr. Weedley, could I speak to you…uh, privately? It seems we have a…uh, *situation*."

Weedley wheels about. "A *situation? We?*"

"Yes, in a manner of speaking."

Industrial arts teacher, Hugh Woods, looks up from where his thumbnail chisels the edge of the table. "Spill it, you're among friends." Hugh's one of those types that would be a hippie if they were still in style.

Miss Sprite adjusts her voice to suit the occasion. "It's just that two senior students, Madeline Murchison and Brad Hanson, have been engaged in a sort of sticky situation."

Weedley shakes his head. "Why they are two of our best students. What kind of sticky situation could they possibly be involved in?"

Miss Ambross, an elderly spinster with forty years of teaching home economics under her belt but little above it, nods. "Why yes, they have certainly set a fine example for the junior students to look up to."

Sprite toys with her whistle. "The students looked up alright, but…"

Weedley wiggles his shoulders into place. "Hmm, exactly what kind of a situation are we looking at here?"

Again Sprite toys with her whistle. "Uh, we didn't. That is, they fell through the ceiling of the auditorium onto the floor while I was giving the junior girls their gym class."

Weedley lurches. "How on earth did *that* happen? Were they injured?"

"Oh no, they're fine. We got the mats under them before they dropped. And they seemed to be able to move quite rapidly once they were down."

Weedley stretches his hands out from the cuffs of his suit jacket and places them on the table. "Thank God for that. No law suits to contend with. Plummer, would you please phone the maintenance office as soon as possible."

Plummer pulls a pen from behind a pearly pink ear and a notebook from the pocket of a pin-stripped powder blue suit-jacket and jots diligently.

Miss Ambrose tilts a frown. "Now what in heaven's name do you suppose they were doing up there?"

"I don't, you see they were naked," Miss Sprite murmurs.

'Naked' although spoken softly, launches Mr. Harmon J. Spencer and his English and History teaching cultivation forward. "Great Caesar!"

Miss Ambrose hides herself behind a muttering voice. "Oh dear, dear, dear."

Weedley's hands shrink into his sleeves, his neck into his collar as he utters, almost imperceptibly, "A sticky situation."

School counselor, Miss Yardley, glances at Ben Dent, and winks. Her cropped hair is secured with a damask headband, while her features, although pleasant, have that lean drawn look of women who jog too much. As for Dent, he isn't what one would call handsome but he has that rakish confidence of a Tom Cruise that women can't resist. Of course, his education would account for his knowledge of the laws of 'bodies in motion' and natures fragile ecological balance, but one can't help but wonder why he's nearing forty and has yet to experience marital bliss.

Mr. Harmon J. Spencer clears his throat and moistens his lips so as to shape his syntax. "Are there no *laws* to discourage such conduct? Gross *in-de-cen-cy*? Statutory *rrrape?*"

The 'rrr' quivers the table top like a struck gong.

Weedley wipes the sweat from is forehead with a sleeve. "Miss Plummer, have you anything to offer with regard to this stic…ah, situation?"

Her pen pokes an indentation in the peach-like surface of a cheek, while her note-pad raps rhythmically on the tabletop. "Point one; they didn't expose themselves voluntarily, thus no gross indecency. Point two; they are both seventeen, thus no statutory rape…and I don't believe sexual intercourse is a crime."

Dent chuckles. "It certainly doesn't seem so at the time."

Mr. Weedley runs a handful of fingers through the tangles of his wooly rust hair. "I'm always open for suggestions. You people know that."

Her embarrassment apparently quelled, Miss Ambrose knits her brow. "Where are they now?"

"They're in the office waiting room," Miss Sprite says.

"What…ah, state are they in at this point in time?" Weedley asks. "Ah, garment-wise, that is."

"Oh, they're fully clothed now."

Weedley adjusts his tie and tucks the tip under his lapel. "Well that's a relief."

"Oh?" Den says.

Mr. Harmon J. Spencer frowns at Dent then coughs impeccably. "I would *think* that our student *coun*selor, Miss *Yard*ley, would have some ad*vice* to offer us relevant to the situ*at*ion at hand. Well, Miss Yardley?"

Yardley nods. "Ah yes, at hand…why yes, there are two basic factors that are instrumental in molding a child's behavioral patterns: hereditary factors: environmental factors."

Dent nods. "Parentally determined, in every case. You see, their parents have in all likelihood participated in sexual activities at sometime or other."

"Let us get *ser*ious, shall we?" Mr. Harmon J. Spencer says. "After all, we *are* people in a respected and responsible position in our society and we are expected to conduct ourselves accordingly. Now what counseling procedures would you recommend, Miss Yardley…cough…in guiding these two youths into a more structured life*style*?"

"A child's behavioral patterns are largely determined by the time they reach adolescence, and furthermore, they may have been participating in this type of activity for sometime."

Dent chuckles. "Why yes, and I'm sure we are *all* aware of what a dastardly difficult habit it is to break oneself of."

"You can say that again," sputters from Hugh's lips.

Weedley fusses himself into place. "Come now, people; let's have some suggestions."

"Maybe you could ground them," Miss Ambrose says.

"Yes, yes, that's good. I like that idea."

Dent nods. "Well, at any rate it would stop them from climbing into high places."

Miss Ambrose's teaching instinct takes over. "No, no, no, Benjamin, you misunderstand me. I was suggesting that they be grounded in the sense of being disallowed extracurricular activities."

Hugh turns sideways in his chair and flops an arm over the back. "Wouldn't work. They'd just have more time for fooling around."

Mr. Harmon J. Spencer head gives a twitch sideways. "Fooling around? If you're referring to…cough…of course, it would be nice…cough…advantageous, if you will, to know con*clus*ively whether or not the party…cough… *couple* in question were actually par*tici*pating in sexual activi*ties*…as a means to better assess the matter, of course."

Dent turns to Miss Sprite. "Did you *see* anything?"

"I didn't actually *see* anything…let me rephrase that…I didn't actually see them *doing* anything…of that…uh, nature."

Dent nods. "But the real 'meat of the issue' is, we only have circumstantial evidence to work with."

"Would that be exhibit one?" Yardley seems interested in knowing.

"The real question is would it stand up in court."

A few quiet chuckles before Hugh says, "There aren't that many reasons why people undress in lofts; that having been said, based on my knowledge of the durability of different structures and materials, I'd estimate that a hell-of-a…" A few chuckles sputter from his lips before he's able to resume. "…plenty of pounding would have to have taken place."

"But," Dent grooming his voice with genuine financial concern. "Due to this breakage of school property, isn't the school board going to be concerned with the 'fucking overhead'?"

This remark ejects Mr. Harmon J. Spencer from this chair like a launched missile. The problem is, once he is erect, the roar of laughter annihilates not only his thoughts on word choice but also his syntax, enunciation and any other aspect of the proper English spoken word he has cultivated. He slumps into his chair like a deflated balloon.

After a moment of silence in which only sporadic sputters of laugher are emitted, Mr. Harmon J. Spencer recovers sufficiently to cough, then scraping his chair into the traditional table-chair-relationship, he says, "Mr. *Dent*, would you kindly re*frain* from your inane attempts at *jocularity*. Activities such as this are in*deed* serious matters and should be *treated* as such."

"Oh, lighten up, H.J.," Hughie says. "Kids will be kids, eh? I imagine you had your escapades when you were young."

Spencer jerks back. "Me! Escapades! Why I nev…cough…" He is silent for a moment then says, "So, does this mean you con*done* such practices?"

"Well, I wouldn't go so far as to say I con…oh, hell, H.J., face facts, shit happens."

"Great Caesar! Is it necessary that educated people succumb to the language of bohemians?"

"Come on now, H.J., a little colloquial dialect always adds colour to a discussion."

Mr. Harmon J. Spencer grips his lapel; gives it a shake. "We are *teach*ers, not rapscallions. Now the point I've been attempting to clarify, if I'm allowed to do so…cough…is precisely *this:* such con*duct* is inex*cus*able in an educational insti*tute*. Would you not a*gree*, Mr. Weedley?"

Weedley jerks on one sleeve at a time. "Personally, I like the counseling idea."

Dent says, "Sex education *is* on the curriculum. And, of course, we *could* consider this incident a little practical experience."

"A sort of job-study?" Yardley asks.

Hughie snorts as he slaps the tabletop. "How about a 'job-entry project'?"

Mr. Harmon J. Spencer's head snaps back stiff-necked. "Great Caesar!" Then he settles his slim fingertips on the tabletop, tap, taping. "Is it not *pos*sible for those present to adopt an adult atti*tude* toward this matter and re*frain* from ridiculing a grave situ*ation*? Now if you'll re*call*, I told all of you when the issue sex education was first dis*cussed*, that when you teach children the fundamental mechanics of sexual communion, it is akin to instructing them how to ride a *bicycle* and then not allowing them to *ride one*. Why at the very first oppor*tun*ity they will jump…"

"I did," Dent says. "Mind you, everything would have been fine and dandy had my foot not slipped off the pedal."

For a moment, a snicker, a snort, a cough meld with thoughtful sips of coffee.

"Well Mr. Waldo Weedley?" asks Mr. Harmon J. Spencer.

"Well what?" asks Weedley.

"What disciplinary measure are you about to introduce?"

"Personally," Weedley says. "I like the counseling idea. What do you think Plummer?"

Miss Plummer's pen rotates in her fingers rapping the tabletop each time the tip comes around. "Let's see now. I suppose it all comes down to the question of whose job is it to raise children. The name, 'teacher', implies that their job lies within the realm of teaching. The name, 'parent', implies that their job lies within the realm of parenting."

Weedley gets to his feet. "Very well put, Plummer. Obviously, this is a parenting issue thus we are free of all responsibility. Phone their parents immediately, Plummer."

"And the name, 'principal', implies that his job lies principally in handling…"

Weedley leans toward her with the support of his knuckles on the tabletop. "And the name, 'Plummer', implies that *her* job could go down the drain if she doesn't abide by my wishes."

Plummer's pen-tip taps her thoughts well into the tabletop before she gets to her feet, spins on a heel and leaves.

Moments later, she returns. "They've gone."

"Good," says Weedley. "Inform the parents of the occurrence and we're rid of the whole sordid mess."

Mr. Harmon J. Spencer drums the tabletop. "And that's it?"

"Well what more do you want…blood?"

"We must send a *mess*age to the other students that this type of…"

The buzzer, clinging to a high corner of the room, rants.

"Time to go." Weedley wheels on a heel and strides toward the door. "Let's sleep on it. By morning, it will all seem *so insignificant*."

The room is vacated. The buzzer is silent. Only an ominous presence lingers: the residual of some recent cataclysmic occurrence.

Dent stops at his classroom door to examine the doorknob

Yardley approaches from behind. "A class now?"

Dent turns. "Yes. Physics 91 awaits me."

"Is that all that awaits you? You seem preoccupied."

"I've been thinking about what went on back there."

"And what do you think about it?"

"Well, what do you think about it?"

"No, no, I'm the counselor."

"Why don't you start being a woman."

"Oh, my, my, my. We *are* touchy this morning, aren't we? Have a bad night?"

"I'm sorry, that was really uncalled for."

"Yes, it was."

"But who wouldn't be touchy after listening to those people?"

"Me. So why should it bother you?"

Dent pulls on an ear lobe. "It didn't bother me. It's just that they treat this type of incident as if it's a catastrophe? Many girls get married at seventeen or younger. Why do you suppose adolescents are fully developed sexually in their early teens: to play ring-around-the-rosy?"

"Now there's a new twist to an old game."

"Can't you get serious?"

Yardley grins. "I'm merely using your technique. But since you want me to be serious, what do you suppose the Murchisons will say when they discuss the phone call they are about to receive?"

"Oh that's easy. Mrs. Murchison will say to her husband, 'Don't worry dear, I've had her on the pill for months now.' Of course, he will say, 'What!' But that will be the end of it."

"Really, and how about the Hansons?"

"Oh, let's see, Mrs. Hanson will say to her husband, 'He needs fatherly guidance, dear. Handle it, handle it.' And he'll simply take Brad aside, pat him on the shoulder and say, 'It is of paramount importance to base each of life's ventures on a solid foundation."

Yardley laughs. "Okay, okay, but tell me, what's really bothering you?"

Cynthia Skinner approaches, dimpling her cheeks with a smile and cuddling a thought with a head tilt. "Good morning, Ben...neee..." She glances at Yardley then at Dent. "Ah...sir."

"Ah, yes...good morning, Cynthia," Dent says, stepping back to glance obliquely at Yardley, who folds her arms, tucks her tongue in a cheek and slowly nods. Dent shrugs before focusing his attention on Cynthia, who gently releases him from her smile and softly brushes past him into the classroom, leaving him to stare at the dark stain of the hardwood door.

Yardley slowly oscillates on a heel. "So, you didn't have a bad night after all."

"I was merely helping the girl with her...ah Physics."

"Really now, Ben...eee..."

Dent twists his earlobe. "A platonic relationship, at best, ah...worst...ah."

" 'Ben...eee' doesn't have a platonic ring to it. You know, Ben...eee, Cynthia must be at least half your age. There are women available closer to your age...closer in proximity, if you'd just open your eyes."

"Age is such a poor measure of maturity."

Yardley nods. "I'll buy that."

"Besides, look at how many famous or rich men marry women years younger than them."

"Marriage, eh? Oh, oh! That gorgeous little number has you clasped so firmly in the palm of her hand that you don't have a ghost of a chance of squeezing out between her fingers. Not that you want to."

"Well, who knows, eh? Who knows where this will lead."

"I know exactly where it will lead. You're going to run into more 'Spencers'. School board. Parents. Many of them not so liberally minded as you. Sorry fella, but you'll be history. Need counseling?"

Dent turns the knob. "Goodbye."

Yardley walks away. "Have a nice day."

The moment Dent enters the hush of the classroom he can sense that lingering presence. But Dent's problem, at least for the moment, is how to teach a class of youths whose hormones are migrating up their arteries like spawning salmon. He picks up a piece of chalk and flips it end over end as he saunters over to the window. Last night's snowfall has transformed the drab world into a wonderland of soft sounds and glittering newness yet beneath the canted window frame an icy chill nips at his knuckles. He turns to the class. "What was last nights homework assignment?"

Cynthia smiles. "The laws governing free falling bodies."

A titter runs through the classroom.

"And can you state the concept?"

"Free falling bodies, regardless of weight, when dropped simultaneously from the same height will reach the ground at the same time. In a vacuum, of course, otherwise we'd have the atmospheric resistance as a factor to be considered."

"I see, but wouldn't the heavier body fall faster?"

"No."

"Why not?"

"Because of gravitational acceleration. The extra force required to accelerate the heavier body counteracts the greater gravitational force."

"Very good, Cynthia."

Dent's about to ask Cynthia which of the two bodies would have the greater impact when it struck the ground, but something written in fine letters in the corner of the blackboard catches his eye.

'Problem; how many eight inch strokes driven by 190 lb. thrusts would it take to break through ¾ inch ceiling tile mounted on ½ inch laths.'

It's Cynthia's work. It has her touch. His eyes turn to Cynthia, in her place at the front of the class: hands interlocked serenely on her desktop: that immunity that only the young possess coyly tucked to one side.

Mr. Dent knows enough not to become angry. Perhaps he should turn it into a joke. "Do any of you have an answer?"

Rob from the back of the class offers. "Wouldn't it depend on the cushioning effect?"

The class applauds.

Cynthia winks at Ben. He gives the chalk one more flip, watches it settle in the palm of his hand then turns to the window. A frosty fork of white clings to an elm limb; a slight atmospheric disturbance and it falls away splitting like a wishbone. The chalk taps lightly on the pane.

The Note

Morley and Elsie Marsh do not stand out at these house parties. At least not to Ray Meyers. Morley's a tall slim man with thin lips that control a no-nonsense mouth. His grey balding head makes him look to be in his fifties rather than forties. Although his wife, Elsie, holds her age well, ten years younger, only slightly taking on that mid-age plumpness, she carries a prudish mien in that facial expression as if things are never quite right. Maybe they aren't, but why should Ray care? The only reason he ever notices them, and this is only a fleeting glance when Ray's wife Joan dances with Morley, is because he doesn't understand why Joan dances with dull, drab Morley when there are handsome sprightly husbands in the crowd.

Ray wakes up Saturday morning to find he's alone in bed. This isn't at all unusual. His wife Joan doesn't linger in bed with him as she did earlier in their marriage. As he slides out of bed on his way to the bathroom, the bright morning sun alights a sharp white corner from a dresser drawer slightly ajar. It's reserved for Joan's panties. Her papers are kept in a drawer in their study downstairs. What's paper doing in there? Ray opens and pulls on the white corner and a note slips out. Silently he reads, '*My dearest Joanie love, the week seems endless until I can once again clasp you to my heart in dance at the party Saturday night and make love to you again Sunday morning. My love for you grows daily as it has from whence we first crossed paths of intimacy. Until then, I hold you in my heart, love of my life, my sweet seducible Joanie, love Morley.*'

"*My* sweet seducible Joanie?' Ray yells. "My trusting friggin' wife being taken in by that straight-laced bastard and his lousy attempt at writing a love note." Ray picks up a framed picture of Joan from his bedside table and hurls it; it catches the bathroom doorjamb shattering the glass and bending the frame. Luckily there are two closed doors between him and the kitchen where he hears Joan clanking pans. Quieting his anger, he mutters, "What the hell, I can't believe this…how long has this been going on. A wife I trusted implicitly…I'm going to beat the hell out that bastard, out of someone, she's just as much to blame, why not tell me she wanted out… or *does* she?" He lies back down on the bed, that is now trembling, and tries to read but the paper won't stay still. "That stupid Morley, skinny insipid Morley, what the hell does she see in that idiot that I can't offer her? I'm going down stairs and tear a strip off her." As he's brushes up the glass and tosses it into a wastebasket, he pauses. *Hey, fella, get hold of your cool, you've got power here, you're in full control of things, there's got to be a much better way to handle this.* Quickly, he replaces the note trying to get it under her panties and in exactly the same position; no easy task with shaking hands. He leaves the drawer opened just the same amount as she did, he thinks. He can't go down stairs and fake not knowing until his hands and mind settle down. A long warm shower will help. He shucks his shorts and steps into the shower. He sets the temperature just right, nice and warm but not too hot. "Geez!" A shot of ice-cold water flipsides that soothing warmth. "Shit, that loyal bitch is running the water in the bathroom down stairs."

It's a good half hour later before Ray can get himself in a state to remain cool and show nothing, he hopes. As he enters the kitchen Joan is sitting at the kitchen table reading through a pile of cookbooks and sipping coffee. Ray goes to the percolator and pours himself one. "Morning sweetheart," he says as he walks over and gives her a peck on a receding cheek. Sure, he's aware of this subtle withdrawing but he wouldn't have noticed yesterday. He skids out a chair and sits down. "What are you going to cook up?"

"Oh, I'm to bring a dessert to the party tonight."

"You know, Joan, I think it would be nice if you and I forgot about the party tonight…"

This raises Joan's eyes from flipping through the recipe books.

"…and went out to the Flopping Flounder Inn By the Sea, and had a gourmet dinner by candlelight and wine, did a little dancing, had a swim in their indoor pool, enjoyed their sauna and spent the night there."

She stares at Ray for a moment. "Well I…I've already promised to take some desert…"

Ray holds his coffee in two hands and stares over its rim at Joan as he continues to sip on his thoughts.

She lowers her eyes to the cookbooks. "…and…uh, besides it's rude… you know, to cancel at short…at the last minute and…"

He stares a frown at her still sipping.

"…besides…"

"What's wrong, Joan, run out of viable reasons?"

"Viable? Why they're all viable."

"Really Joan?" Ray gets to his feet briskly; firmly fixes this question on her for a moment then turns and leaves the room. He goes to his den, closes the door and mixes a scotch and soda. He tries to read but can't concentrate. *Maybe I should have been inviting her to do things like I suggested a long time ago. Maybe now it wouldn't help anyway. What's the point…thinking about what's done…it can't be undone. It's too late; my trust, my love, it's all been violated.* "Shit!" he mutters, as his irrational thoughts ricochet around the room only to bounce back to annihilate any rational thoughts that try to surface. As he pauses to pour another scotch, he hears her footsteps on the stairs; across their bedroom floor; silence then something slams or is dropped. Could be the bathroom door, it could be something dropped, or it could be her slamming her panty drawer.

The second scotch slows the thoughts and eases him into a rational state of mind, he thinks. *Sure, we'll go to the party, me as an observer; obviously things have been going over my head at these social gatherings.*

There's a light knock on the door of his den. "Can I come in?"

"If you want."

Joan opens the door, somewhat timidly. "You're drinking very early. You must be upset."

He says nothing but sips.

Joan sits down in a swivel chair at his desk and swings to face him. "Could I have one too?"

Without a word, he pours her a scotch and hands it to her.

She takes an ample drink. "Maybe we could have the dinner and then go to the party."

"No, no, there is *no* middle road."

"I've just been thinking, it was a nice idea you suggested….maybe…"

"No, it was a stupid idea, I mean really, this lovey-dovey nonsense at our age."

"No, it was a…a sweet…I…" Joan pauses, to bite back tears.

"No I changed my mind, I *want* to go to the party; they're a lot more fun than…"

"I…I'm sorry, Ray. I spoiled your sweet thought…I…"

"Forget it." Ray gets to his feet. "Make your cheesecake, I'm going for a long walk"

As he turns the corner of Tenth and Maple, he heaves a sigh. *I'm just going to play it cool and observe starting tonight. Then I'll know what to do. Damn it she seemed sincere…sorry…now don't go soft fella, she's been cheating on you and obviously doesn't want to stop.*

Ray and Joan arrive at the party a bit late; the air is filled with the stench of smoke and alcohol and voices ringing joviality as the mix of socializing is in full swing. Ray leaves Joan to take her cheesecake to the kitchen. He gets himself a scotch and soda, finds an isolated spot to silently sit and sip. When Joan returns, she makes the rounds talking; laughing; affectedly; excessively with one couple then another while maintaining a calculated distance from Morley, who is doing the same on the other side of the room. Someone turns on some up-tempo music for the early dancing; slow dreamy music will come as the evening draws on. Joan accepts a dance courteously offered by the host, Les Craig, as he makes *his* rounds. A glance her way by Morley and he requests a dance from Susan North. Some couples dance with their spouses, others choose randomly, or so it would seem, while others continue tipping drinks in conversation. When the majority of those present are dancing, Joan and Morley dance together: casually of course, while mixing dancing with others.

The evening draws on and dinner's consumed. Perhaps minds are dimmed enough that Morley and Joan can dance with the subtle tenderness of casual conversation; of daily trivia that only has meaning to those in love. They do. But it's only later, when lights dim and music slows; shoes kicked off; hair let down; and the hazy ambience permeates booze dimmed minds, do Joan and Morley risk more intimate dancing. Through the smoky haze of dancers, when Joan's face turns, her features are as bland as a marble statuette's. But once, when facing away, Ray catches a glimpse of her features flashing a vibrant smile at Morley in the mirror above the sideboard; and then there's Morley's hand placed well below the small of Joan's back. And yes, Joan *is* loved by another man.

Are others aware? Along the floor line of hassocks, cushions, sofa legs, head-shadows turn in furtive hesitancy to watch, or purposely not watch, what they have been aware of all along through that clear vision of the detached. The truth was there; a social secret exchanged among friends yet floating teasingly just beyond Ray's reach; lightly bouncing off the outside of his bubble of trust clouded by his naivety. They all have known; this is what hurts; this is what's unforgivable. Does Elsie exist in such a bubble? If so, all Ray has to do is pop it. If not, she's available waiting for the taking, for he, is completely free of guilt and refute.

He looks across the room to where Elsie's in deep conversation with Carol Barnes and Teresa Stanley; all three sitting on the floor in the shade of a fake palm tree. Floating on his newly acquired knowledge of how affairs are managed, Ray strolls over, and rather smartly, glides to the floor nearby. Elsie gives him a glance, as the others do, before they continue their conversation. Leaning back against a sofa leg, he observes the dancers knowing that he is now fair game for the ladies, especially Elsie.

"Personally," Elsie says. "I think they were fools to change the decor. People liked it as it was."

"If it works," Ray says, without looking their way. "Don't fix it."

"Exactly," Elsie says, stealing a sideways glance at Ray.

"Well, I don't care *what* you say," Carol says, her eyes sidling as if to look at Ray but not quite. "If you don't try something *new* then you won't get change."

"Change for better or worse?" Ray asks, still watching the dancers.

"Well, how are *you* going to know if *you* don't try someon…uh. something different?" Teresa says, looking directly at Ray.

He feels he could actually choose amongst these three, however, the husbands of the other two appear to be remaining faithful. Or are they merely better at concealing it?

Ray gets to his feet. "Exactly, let's dance, Elsie."

He takes her hand and pulls her off the hassock. Actually, he didn't *need* to pull. Ray's amazed at her readiness stripped of primness, exuding vivaciousness. And as they come together, her perfect fit.

This might not be such a difficult task after all. We'll just see if a little jealousy can be aroused. "I suppose I was rude interrupting your conversation with the other ladies?"

"Not at all, it was a standoff argument anyway. I wasn't giving an inch and neither were they, thanks for the support."

Ray draws his head back to look at her. "Sometimes in our lives we have need for support."

Elsie gazes back at Ray with a thoughtful nod. "Support? Yes, or a change."

"You're nice to dance with, Elsie, you seem to fit; to move so nicely with me."

"Fit? Why yes, you fit…ah, nicely…ah, into me."

"Mm hmm."

Loraine Craig comes in from the kitchen with a tray of small sandwich wedges and sets it on the coffee table. Jan Price follows with a tray of cold cuts, cheese and olives. May Mosley follows with small saucers, napkins and petite two prong forks, and…oh yes, cheesecake.

"Not more food," Ray says. "Hungry, Elsie?"

"Yes, I didn't feel like eating dinner."

"Me neither. How about me getting us a couple of saucers and some goodies and us sitting on the floor in that dark corner under the fake willow tree and us having ourselves a cosy little pick-nick." Ray winks at Elsie.

"And I'll replenish our drinks." Elsie winks back as she leaves for the bar.

Shortly, Ray and Elsie are sitting close and cosy in the darkened corner nibbling goodies and sipping drinks. "Hey this is fun, eh Elsie?"

"Yes, it's almost like having a real pick-nick."

"But with an ambience of naughtiness like children skipping school."

"Or us skipping marriage."

They exchange smiles and laughter. "But you know, Elsie, our park has shade trees that aren't fake and shrubbery that can provide privacy for those who desire…*it.*"

"Why not a walk on the beach arriving at that little pub when it opens at eleven. They have rooms to let up stairs; I like comfort."

"Best offer I've had in months."

Across the room, Joan and Morley have awakened from their close contact reverie to notice. Joan says something to Morley, who shrugs then tilts his head toward the goodies. As they move toward the coffee table Joan glances over at Ray. He wouldn't have seen this without the help of the reflective surface the china cabinet beyond them. She isn't pleased with this. Ray's mind chuckles silently: maliciously: *the disloyal bitch, and me, obviously the only one in this place that didn't know.*

Ray doesn't press things further this particular night, he feels he holds the winning hand and so he's playing it cool. At the end of the evening, when he sees Morley get Elsie's coat from the rack and Joan standing waiting for him to get hers, he gets to his feet and pulls Elsie to hers. "At ten thirty?"

"Exactly."

Next morning, Joan says, "I suppose you'll do your usual jogging in the park while I'm playing tennis with the girls."

"Or I may play tennis with the boys. There are plenty of courts available there."

"They'll all be spoken for."

Ray winks at Joan. "Well, I'd rather joggle anyway."

She frowns at this.

Being Sunday morning, the pub is quiet with only a hushed drone, the aftermath of a Saturday night binge or love affair. As for Elsie and Ray, they haven't started theirs as yet. With beer mugs in hand they sip and gaze at each other. Ray tells Elsie about Morley's love note to Joan.

"The bastard."

"A week ago this time," Ray says, "I was jogging in the park and believing I had a decent marriage."

Elsie shakes her head. "Decent, oh fine, Raymond, what more could a person want than a descent marriage, eh?"

"How long have you known?"

"Since it started, I'm not like you Ray, I don't trust as readily, I watch, I see. Either you were blinded by trust or not paying attention because you didn't really care that much."

"Then why did the note anger me so much?"

"Because, a trick had been played on you and when you realized everyone was in on it, you were embarrassed and humiliated."

"Why haven't you confronted Morley about it?"

"Because, Raymond, I just don't care."

"Did you ever love him?"

"Yes, when I was young because he adored me and showed it?"

"So why don't you care now?"

"Because being adored is nice but it's not enough. I have to love a man for what he is."

"Yes, I guess that's why I never showered Joan with all that flattery stuff, I didn't think it was the important part of a relationship. Anyway, what do you plan on doing?"

Elsie reaches over and places her hand on Ray's. "Well, Raymond, let see how this turns out."

"Have you ever had an affair before Elsie?"

"No."

"Me neither, I'm not comfortable with it at all: I find it illicit "

"Meaning?"

"Like I'm cheating on Joan, my marriage, on something."

"Hmm, strange after what they've been doing, but I get a feeling like that too, actually I'm a little scared."

"Me too. Maybe, we should just put this off until…"

"When?"

"I don't know, I guess until we find out how this will go."

"It won't go anywhere unless we make it go somewhere. Getting a room up stairs seems like a good place to start."

They're in the room now, standing and looking at each other as if they haven't the foggiest notion of the proper protocol in conducting an affair.

"Well," Ray says.

"Well, you're the man. It's always the man who starts affairs isn't it?"

"How would I know, I've never started one and I've never been a woman."

"Well, how do you start it with Joan?"

"But that's not an affair, there must be a, I don't know; a subtle or romantic something to make it special, I would think. How do you two start it at home?"

"We don't anymore."

Ray takes the initiative and steps over to the bed. "Okay, let's get in bed."

"Taking some clothes off might be a good place to start, Raymond."

"Oh yes, I suppose it would be proper to take at least something off."

"Yes, it might be necessary eventually anyway. You first."

"Hmm, the way you're acting, you'd think you'd never undressed in front of any guy other than Morley."

"I haven't. Have you ever undressed in front of any other woman than Joan?"

"No."

"Well?"

"Okay, I'll start." Ray slips his jogging shirt over his head.

"Fantastic start," Elsie says with a chuckle. "Come on sport, take it off, take it off, or are you chicken?"

"No one calls *me* chicken." Ray sheds clothing until he drops his shorts to his feet and kicks them at her with a toe. "There you go babe, what do you think?"

Elsie catches them and tosses them away. "Oh my God, sport, and Joan left *that* for Morley's shorty."

"Shut up, it's your turn."

Elsie sheds and as she kicks her panties at Ray off a toe. "I don't need to ask what *you* think of mine."

Shortly, they're in bed and well on their way into their own creative protocol.

"Oooo," Elsie utters. "Speaking of a good place to st...st...art, ooo my goodness, Ray, you're ga...ga...good at this."

A couple of hours later, they are sitting in the pub having a meltdown with beer and fish and chips.

"You know what I think, Raymond?"

Ray stops a julienne just before his teeth. "What?"

"I believe we are sexually compatible."

"I'd be compelled to agree. But where does that leave us?"

"Cripes, Raymond, do I have to make all the decisions?"

"No, but the last one was so good, I thought I'd give you first chance."

"Let's just leave it like this until next Saturday's party and see how it goes. And next Sunday do this again, unless something significant happens between now and then."

The following Saturday, the Marshes are already at the party when the Meyers arrive. Joan hustles off to the kitchen with another cheesecake while Ray scans the room; Morley's near the bar talking to Fred Bradley; with his wallet in hand, apparently about to buy drinks. Ray hustles by unnoticed and buys two Bacardi and Sevens. He walks over to where Elsie has been sitting talking to Pamela Strand and hands her one, here love."

"Oh, Raymond, why thank you. You knew my drink."

"Of course, love."

This raises Pam's eyebrows.

"Sorry to interrupt your conversation ladies, I'll see you later Elsie."

"Yes, Raymond."

"Mm hum, so Elsie, is it get even time?" Pam asks.

"Getting even doesn't enter the picture, this is naturally grown, you know, organically grown.

"Oh well, well, I see. This should be interesting."

"It already is."

Ray has been sipping and watching when Elsie approaches him. "Enough watching, Raymond, it's time to dance."

She intertwines her fingers into his just as Joan and Morley are. He lets his hand slip down to where Morley's is on Joan. Morley's obviously had his hand all over Joan's bare butt, not that he hasn't done the same with Elsie's, but why not drop his down further too?

"Oh my, my, Raymond, aren't you afraid someone will notice?"

"I know they will."

Elsie laughs.

And so the remainder of the evening unfolds in much the same manner.

Joan is silent as they drive home. It isn't until she pours them each a Drambuie, that she says anything. "You were drinking pretty heavy tonight, to say nothing of you're cosy dancing. You'd think you could have used a little discretion; been more subtle about it." She walks over to the kitchen table where Ray is sitting and sets his drink before him.

"We were emulating."

"So you know."

"Might as well, everyone else has for some time. And why didn't I? Naïve? Stupid? No, I trusted you so much I wasn't looking for it."

Joan scrapes out a chair and sits across the table from Ray. "I'm sorry."

"Sorry doesn't really cut it, Joan." Ray drains the small glass in one swig. "It's not nearly good enough."

"And what is?"

"Nothing now, it's over, it's too late. So why in hell did you do it?"

"Because he adores me."

I need a coffee or something. Hell, I don't know what I need." Ray gets to his feet and turns on the coffee percolator. "Well, you just might be interested in knowing that *I* adore you; I always have."

Joan stares at her miniature glass of Drambuie: dark inside its fragile shell. "But he shows me that he does."

"Oh yes indeed, with poorly written love notes and his hand on your ass." As Ray looks at Joan and says this, he pours coffee, some of which goes into his cup; the rest runs along the counter top and dribbles on the floor. "Of course, I have no idea what other ways he has of showing you."

"So you found the note?"

"Yes."

"You shouldn't have been snooping."

Ray walks back to his chair. "You left your panty drawer half opened and the sun was shining on this white corner of paper. 'What,' I asked myself, 'is paper doing in my trusting wife's panty drawer; she is always *so* particular about keeping her paperwork in the drawer of her desk in the study'."

Still staring at her glass, Joan asks, "Could you write better ones?"

"Hah, wouldn't be difficult."

"Then why don't you?"

"Oh for Christ sakes Joan, no man writes love letters to his wife."

"Maybe they should; maybe they should make their wives feel special like they did when they first met, rather than a damned servant to have babies and look after the house and meals; make them feel like they are still loved in a very special way."

Ray pauses, "Oh my God, I thought that was all understood."

"You know, Ray, when you're having mood swings, puffed up with a baby, in labour in the hospital, kids fighting, suppers burning and a husband coming home wondering why supper isn't ready, it's freakin' hard to remember something that's supposed to be understood."

"And so rather than tell me, you chose to do this."

"You wouldn't have understood and you still don't know the feelings a woman has."

"I don't?"

"No. You're the kind who has to have been there to understand. You don't have enough insight to see things from another's perspective."

"So that's it? Just because he shows he adores you, you've chosen to shack up with him?"

"No, it's that I love him because he adores me."

"And shows it."

"Yes, he's continually telling me and showing me that he adores me."

"So why are you still with me?"

"Because I love you too."

"Why?"

"I don't know."

"Great, that solves a lot."

Later, when Joan gets in bed she faces away from Ray. He lays on his back staring at the darkness of the ceiling until a passing car sends fingers of light around the room and across the drawer, slightly ajar, in which Joan keeps her panties.

Our marriage is through. Every time she'd walk out that door, I'd be wondering. That's not good enough but what? The kids are on their own leading their own lives. Oh sure, they want their parents to stay together but for their own happiness, but they'll adjust. It's happening all the time. Why choose Elsie just because she's Morley's wife? Of course, I'm not making a commitment with her. I will look further.

"Where are you going?" Joan asks Ray next morning

"Jogging while you're playing tennis with the girls."

"But, I'm not going to this morning."

"Why you've been doing it for months?"

"I thought it might be nice if I phoned the Marshes and invited them over to have a little meeting. You know, the four of us."

This catches Ray a little off guard. This is something he should have been saying; not Joan.

"Nice?" he asks.

"Well?" she asks.

"Why not?" he says.

The Marshes arrive at ten for the meeting. Ray opens the door to its ringing.

"Oh how nice to see you this morning," Ray says "Do come in, do come in. Joan informed me that we are going to have a nice meeting. Meetings are nice things to have, amongst close friends"

Morley says nothing as Ray let's him pass. Elsie head tilts a shrug to Ray as she passes.

Once they are seated with a glass of wine in the front room, Ray says, "I understand that one of us, other than myself, wanted this nice meeting called for a specific reason of which I haven't the slightest idea. But if it's going to be so nice, why do I feel like punching someone? Anyway, that aside, would one of you care to fill me in on the matter?"

Morley coughs. "Why yes, Joan…" He looks to Joan, as if for confirmation; he gets a little nod.

"Well, you see, I…that is she…we would like to stop all this foolishness and get back to our normal married life with our own spouses."

"I see," Ray says. "What do you think about that, my dearest Elsie? Our normal married life is how the man phrased it."

"Well, when you borrow something and use it extensively there's a certain amount of depreciation on it that should be compensated for. Don't you think, my sweet Raymond?"

"Why yes, when you cross paths of intimacy and clasp them to your heart in dance, with hand on ass, the depreciation becomes extensive, wouldn't you agree, Elsie my love?"

"Why yes, so to make the agreement fair, would you two, meaning Morley and Joan, tell us how long your affair has been going on?"

"Well," Joan says. "It's difficult to say."

"I imagine," Ray says.

"Well," Morley says, "To be perfectly honest…"

"How many?" Elsie asks.

Joan tosses a hand toward Morley. "Oh why not tell them, Morley; fourteen."

"Hmm," Elsie says. "Makes our one time effort seem rather pitiful, eh Raymond?"

"Didn't feel pitiful."

"That's true, it felt marvellous. But the only fair way is for you two to abstain from sex for thirteen and a half months while we catch up then by that time Ray and I should know if we want to return to our normal married life or divorce you two and get married to each other."

"Excellent idea, Elsie love, and certainly fair."

Morley looks at Joan; Joan looks at Morley; Morley looks at Ray. "I don't like the abstain clause."

"It wasn't inserted in there for you to like," Ray says. "I didn't like that badly written love note that some stupid bastard gave my wife and she hid under her panties in her dresser drawer; or did you hide it there, Morley?"

Joan bunches her brows at Ray. "Like I said before, Ray, you had no business being in my panty drawer."

"I didn't get in it, I merely reached in looking for a pair that would fit."

Elsie and Ray burst out with laughter

"What happened Morley, you were so in love with Joan when you wrote that note and now you want to drop her?"

"It's her idea."

Ray's head swings around. "You're idea Joan?"

"Yes, sweetheart."

"Uh…really?"

"Yes, love."

"Why?"

There's a soft loving tone to Joan's voice that Ray hasn't heard in a long, long time. "Like I told you before sweetheart, because I'm so in love with you."

"Oh come on now, Joan, after what you've done you expect me to swallow that?"

Joan smiles warmly as she says softly, "Why yes, honey, because it's the truth."

There's something in her eyes that's slowly soothing Ray's anger. Oh sure, he'd like to stay angry and he has a damned good reason to, but it's weakening. "But how will I know when you leave the house that you won't do this again?"

"You told me that you adored me, right honey?"

"Well…uh, yes, I…I did."

"All you have to do is show it." Joan gives a cute little head dip and sweet smile. "A few spontaneous words of endearment; an unexpected loving kiss; a little love note with a single rose picked up on the way home to supper; little things like that every so often. Is that too difficult to do?"

Ray shakes his head. "Damn you anyway, Joan, cut that out."

She dips her head slightly and nibbles her lower lip. "What, sweetheart?"

"You know damned well what, I never could say no to that look."

"Well, is it too difficult now, honey, to do those things?"

Ray frowns at Joan.

Joan hands Ray a pen and pad. "You said you could write a better love note than Morley did, sweetheart, let's see if you can."

Ray glances around as if searching for a way out of this nice little meeting. He must find none, so he gazes at Joan for moment then writes. The others wait for his creative results. When his pen stops, Ray tears the page from the pad and hands it to Joan.

Joan reads it aloud

"I'll never forget when we first met,

So young we were, afraid, but yet,

A single rose within our heart,

Soon grew to assure we'd never part."

Ray and Joan come together in a tender embrace.

Elsie and Morley get to their feet; walk quietly across the room and out the door; it clicks shut.

Identical Twins

Todd's having a muffin and coffee at Supreme Coffee Nook in the Crescent Valley Mall while making notes in his notepad when he looks up and sees her. She's just come in the door. There's a string of customers in the line-up but the Nook staff handles the orders quickly. The only problem is that the tables get filled in a hurry. She's a nice looking girl about his age, not beautiful but has very pleasant nicely proportioned features and a trim figure that is neatly dressed with medium priced clothing. Long light brown hair glistens well past her shoulders and she carries herself with an air, certainly not egotistical, but self-assured. The way she walks as the line moves forward, the way she poses each time it stops, the way she tilts her head and knits her brow forming tiny crows-feet around her eyes, casts an ambience of quality, poise and, of course, attractiveness.

As for Todd himself, there's nothing about his medium brown hair or medium blue eyes or the contour of his nose or the set of his jaw that would turn a girl off, but on the other hand, these features offer nothing that would cause her to flip her lid over him either. He's just your common garden-variety male of mid-twenties sitting in his light blue slacks and white shirt while jotting in his notepad.

As the line in front of her shortens, she keeps looking around for an empty seat. With only two customers to go, the only seat available is the one across from Todd at his table. She raises her eyebrows at him and then dips a stare at the seat. He nods to her and hangs his jacket on the back of it. She smiles and nods a thank you.

When her order is filled, she walks her tray over and places it on the table. "Thank you so much. I get my coffee break every day at ten and this place fills up *so fast* I usually can't find an empty spot."

He nods. "Hi, I'm Todd, pleased to be of help."

Lifting her cup of coffee and saucer with a bagel and cream cheese off the tray, she sits down. Several minutes pass by as she meticulously spreads the cream cheese on her bagel. He takes a sip of coffee and continues to write in his note pad. She's munching on her bagel when he looks up to say, "You work here in the mall then?"

"Yes, I'm a receptionist in the clinic."

He picks up his muffin and takes a bite. Then setting it down, he scratches his head and writes a bit more.

"And you?" she asks.

He looks up as if surprised. "Me?"

"Yes, do you work in the mall?"

"Oh, no." He continues to make notes.

She stops chewing to giggle. "It appears that you work *here*."

He looks up. "Pardon?"

"You seem to be very busy as if you're working right now."

"Oh, yes, I suppose it looks that way." He laughs quietly. "I guess I am but I should be more friendly. That's the trouble with people these days, they're so into working making money."

"Yes, that's right. People should slow down and…"

"Smell the rose, right?"

She nods. "Or smell their muffin."

He chuckles lightly. "Hmm, if we're going to visit a little, I should know your name. I'm afraid to talk to strangers."

She laughs a little. "Oh sure, Sharon."

"You like your job at the clinic?"

"It's a job and you do get to meet people, although mostly sick."

He looks at his watch. "Oh, I must go, but I'll tell you what, I come in here often and usually early so I miss the rush. If I see you in the line up I'll save a seat for you."

"Oh, thank you. See you again then."

He nods and leaves.

Several days later, Todd is at Supreme Coffee Nook reading The Crescent Valley Chronicle. He has already hung his jacket over the back of the seat across from him in case Sharon comes in. Of course, he is too engrossed in the financial pages to notice her until she sets her tray down. "Thanks for saving me a seat again, Todd.".

He looks up from his newspaper. "Oh hi, ah, I'm sorry, I've forgotten your name."

"Sharon." After taking everything off the tray, she lifts her coffee. "It's been a couple of days since you've been here. At least around ten."

"Yes, I don't always have a chance to take a coffee break. And then sometimes I go to the pub, depending on who I'm with and the situation."

She holds her coffee with two hands to sip, then holding it slightly away from her lips, she says, "Hmm, I see, it is handy, I'm mean convenient, if you *are* here. Like having a place to sit and someone nice to…ah, well, you know, to talk to."

He shakes the wrinkles out of the newspaper and folds it neatly setting it down beside his crumb sprinkled saucer. "Were you able to find a seat… let's see, it was Monday when I was last here. So Tuesday and Wednesday you weren't able to find seating?"

"Tuesday I stood for five minutes waiting for an old couple to get up. They'd already finished eating and drinking but sat there looking at me as it they wondered why I was standing there. Then the old guy had to go to the washroom and she waited, and Wednesday I had to sit across from one of those street guys. He stunk and kept staring at me."

"Well, if you didn't look so nice maybe he wouldn't have."

She frowns a questioning stare at Todd. "Oh, I guess that's a compliment, why thank you."

Todd chuckles. "You don't recognize a compliment when you hear one?"

"I…hmm, it hit me from a sort of an odd angle" She giggles quietly. "But do you mind telling me what you do?"

Todd leans back and smiles warmly. "Not at all, I play golf and ski when the season and my schedule allows me. I go…"

Sharon raises her long curled up lashes at him. "I meant your job."

"Oh, I work at a hotel."

"Which hotel?"

"Say you're an inquisitive lady, aren't you?"

"You don't need to answer if you don't want to, I was just making conversation."

"I see, okay, I'm the manager of the Crescent Valley Hotel Complex, which includes the pub and wine and beer store. How's that?"

Sharon just sits and gazes at him for a while, then says, "I suppose that'll do…but you're different than most guys I've talked to."

"Good, I like to be an individual." He takes a minute to study her. "So I'm different, just how am I different?"

"To begin with you compliment me as if you're on the make, but you don't try to impress me, you know, elaborate on the money you make and the prestige of the job. A lot of guys would make a big deal out if it to impress me, but you draw back into your notepad or newspaper as if you hardly know I exist."

"Hmm, I sorry, I'm very *much* aware of your existence, you're a charming young lady, but my mind has been so preoccupied by this expansion I'm contemplating with the hotel complex that little else is in my mind. I should take more time to be friendly with people, after all that's all that really counts for anything in this world, right?"

"Exactly." She glances up at the clock on the wall. "Oh gosh, I must go. See you next time, toodle."

It's the third time she's come for coffee break and he's saved her a seat. She walks over and sits her tray down. "Thanks again."

He looks up from his newspaper. "Oh hi, no problem. And how are you doing these days."

"Hmm, okay I guess, sometimes the job gets a little boring but I can't complain."

He gazes at her for a moment, bites his lip with a slight mouth twist. "Do you mind me asking you if you're attached?"

"Attached? Why no, go ahead."

"Well are you?"

She glances around beside her and behind her on the seat. "Hmm, I don't seem to be." Then she gives him a straight on gaze and sniggers. Those cute little crows-feet form around the deep blue of her eyes.

He laughs. "I'm getting too personal, aren't I, sorry."

"I have a steady boy friend, Rob's his name." She looks down and picks up her bagel. She takes her time to spread the cream cheese evenly before biting into it.

"Dating him long?"

"Oh about two years." After a short spell of chewing, she pauses. "You don't have your notebook today."

He raises his eyes from reading the newspaper lying beside him. "Yes, I only bring it when I have something to figure out."

She is still able to talk with a small mouthful, but it makes her lips form a neat little rosebud. "I have things to figure out but I don't use notepads, I do it in my head."

Todd nibbles on a cinnamon roll. "I see, so what are you trying to figure out in your head today?"

"I'm trying to figure you out. You asked if I was attached so it would seem you're interested in me but you don't come on strong like most guys do."

"If a lady's spoken for, I lay off. I'm not into breaking up a couple's relationship. I don't operate that way in love or business. It's not the way the game should be played."

"I was right, you *are* different; you have integrity." She smiles at Todd. "So you have nothing to figure out today, then, eh?"

"Nothing really important anyway?"

She's finished her bagel and slaps her hands together to get rid of imaginary crumbs, wipes her fingers and lips with a napkin to wipe off imaginary cream cheese. Then setting the cup and saucer in the tray, she says, "Must go, see you next time you're here to save me a seat." She gets up and leaves.

"No problem, bye now."

"Toodle," she says smiling and wiggling a few fingers at him.

It's after work on Thursday and Todd has finished a trying meeting with the hotel staff. He saunters out of the conference room almost slumping. Not good for a young man of his age. He needs a woman to come home to, the right kind of woman, to soothe his soul when the day is done. Or he needs a different lively-hood. At this point in time he just wants to relax with a beer. The pub is designed with a Mexican décor with those large heavy hardwood tables and chairs. They're bulky and cumbersome but cushioned in deep leather to provide the comfort for those who spend many hours consuming large quantities of beer. The interior is designed with natural wood that looks like its been torn off some old farm outbuildings, torched, sandblasted and varnished to give it that new rustic appearance.

The barmaid walks over. "Hi Todd, the usual?"

"Hey, Tess, surprise me tonight. Just something on tap."

"I could surprise you other ways if you'd give me a chance."

"I'll think on that, okay?"

"Okay." Her parting movement leaves only a mild wake.

Tess returns and places a pint of pale ail in front of Todd and sits down. "Things are kind of slow right now, is it okay if I sit with you for a second?"

"Sure Tess, you're my best barmaid, you're entitled to take it easy during slack periods."

"What bothers me, Todd, is that you have half a dozen of us girls wanting to date you but you go on being a loner, it's not healthy for a guy your age, we're concerned and would like to help you. Don't you care for women?"

Todd laughs. "I adore women. It's just that I've been really busy, a lot on my mind business wise and I haven't run across the right woman."

"So why does it have to be the right one? You can have a lot of fun with casual female friends and you know it's important to satisfy your sexual appetite. What's wrong with a little recreational sex?"

"Then they lay a heavy on you, you know, they want it to be more than that and then you have a messy situation." From the corner of his eye, Todd's vaguely aware that a couple is working their way through the maze of tables to the one directly behind Tess and him.

Tess says, "I wouldn't."

Todd isn't aware of who's behind him until a hand touches his shoulder. He turns. "Oh Sharon, what are *you* doing here?"

Tess stands to serve them and Todd holds out a hand to stop her. "Wait a second Tess."

Sharon laughs. "Why? Aren't you looking for customers?"

"Why of course, but come on over to my table and I'll get you two a round of drinks and whatnot. Tess, bring the usual for this type of situation, please."

As he moves to sit at Todd's table, Rob turns to watch Tess as she scoots away. Sharon doesn't seem to notice Rob checking Tess out; maybe she doesn't care for she's busy smiling at Todd. "How cool meeting you some place other than the Coffee Nook."

"It happens to people sometimes. I see it happen in here a lot."

Todd and Sharon share a laugh, the humour of which seems to have escaped Rob. He merely sits down and stares at Todd, for a reason Todd's not aware of or cares.

"So you're Rob," Todd says, extending a hand. "Pleased to meet you."

They shake and Rob nods. He's a plain looking guy with a close cropped crescent shaped beard that stretches from ear to ear giving the appearance that he forgot to shave, which may well be the case.

Sharon smiles warmly at Todd. "I saw you sitting here and thought you might be alone so we came over to say hello. Thanks for inviting us to your table. That's really sweet of you."

"You're welcome."

"I assume you're alone, but the barmaid was sitting with you, right?"

Todd laughs. "She'll do that often seeking fringe benefits."

Sharon crinkles her eyes. "Meaning what I think you mean?"

Todd laughs. "Yes."

"It must be hell to be rich and popular."

"But not with the right ones."

Then Sharon turns to Rob. "You remember me mentioning about Todd saving me a seat for my coffee break at The Nook, wasn't that nice of him?"

Rob gives a slow nod. "Oh yeah, very nice, and *every time*."

Sharon crinkles crows-feet at Todd. "Well, Todd, how's business going for you; I see you don't a have your notepad tonight."

"Just finished a stressful meeting in the conference room. I need to unwind."

"Want to talk about it?"

"No thanks Sharon, I want to forget about it, but thanks for being concerned. So what have you two been up to?"

"Oh not that much. Rob's a good golfer, wants to take me golfing but I've never played."

Todd laughs. "Maybe he'll have enough patience to teach you. It's very frustrating when you're learning but once you catch on, it's fun, right Rob?"

Rob nods without smiling.

Then Tess returns with another barmaid carrying four platters. They slip the items off the trays; a jug of beer and four glasses; buffalo wings; nachos; calamari; potato skins. "Will that be all?" Tess asks, holding the trays under an arm. She looks at Rob and winks then turns to leave with the other barmaid following her.

"Now don't be shy guys, " Todd says. "They're on the house, in a manner of speaking."

Tess returns before Todd has time to dip his nacho chip into the salsa. She leans toward Todd and says quietly. "The manager's been giving me a rough time for sitting and talking with you and he's a bit upset with how you treated Gomes in the meeting."

Todd smiles at Tess. "You can sit here any time you want to Tess. You're an excellent employee. Go back to the bar and tell him I want to talk to him."

"Okay."

Rob and Todd watch her cheeky departure. Sharon says, "You guys, can't keep your eyes of a girl's butt."

"Why should we?" Todd asks. "No one criticizes a person for gazing at a beautiful sunset, eh Rob?"

Rob nods as he shoves a salsa loaded nacho chip between his teeth.

Todd is chewing on a sprig of calamari when the manager walks over. He's an obese middle-aged man with a cigar stuck in his mouth. It doesn't appear to be lit but that's fine because there's no smoking in this area.

"Sit down and have a beer, Les," Todd says. Todd takes a swig of his pale ail then says, "These are friends of mine, Sharon and Rob, and I'm treating them to some goodies and then I'm taking then into the restaurant for steak and lobster. Do you have any idea Les, why I'm doing this?"

Sharon and Rob sit staring at Todd as if he is about to disclose some intriguing mystery. Les, who has just been swilling his beer sets it down and shakes his head.

"Well, it's because I like them. They're very nice people and I really like very nice people and I'm a very generous man to people I like. Now you take Gomes, for example, he's not a generous man and there's only one person he likes and so I chose to tell him so. I'm not very nice to those that I don't like and are skinflints. Do you see what I'm getting at, Les?"

"Yes, yes, I get the point." He gets up quickly and leaves.

Todd heaves a sigh. "As soon as I find an good wife, I'm going to sell this whole bloody issue and lead a good clean family life." He winks at Sharon. Rob frowns. "I've had enough of this for one evening, I want to enjoy my ail with my nice friends here. Leave a little room because we're going into the restaurant for steak and lobster and I've got a little jazz trio that plays nice mellow music that we can dance to if we want."

"Oh," Sharon says, "I love lobster but never can afford it, and I love jazz too."

"So how about you, Rob, what kind of music do you like?"

"Country music, you know, The Hag, The Out Laws."

"Oh sure, nice music."

"Yeah, that's the crowd, great music."

"Sure it is, all types of music have their place and their followers, eh Sharon?"

"Yes Todd, but tell me, Tess called that man the manager, I thought you told me you were?"

"I lied, I own the damned place."

Robs eyes bug and so does Sharon. "You own it?"

"Yes won the whole nine yards, Hotel Complex, Pub, Wine and Beer Store in a box of corn flakes, but this set-up's getting to be a pain in the ass. I feel like selling the whole thing and starting a chicken ranch in Combs."

"Box of corn flakes?" Rob says slopping his mug of beer.

Sharon shakes her head. "He's just joking, Rob. But really, Todd, I had no *idea* you were so *important*."

"Important? Importance is in the eye of the beholder."

"Isn't that supposed to be love, Todd?"

Todd fixes his eyes on Sharon's that shine back with those deep blue shades of something special. "Yes, love."

Sharon ducks her gaze away for a moment then picks up a buffalo wing. As she munches on it a small smear of sauce blemishes the soft texture of her cheek. Todd picks up a napkin, reaches across the table and gently wipes it off. "Now you're perfect."

Sharon flutters those long curled-up lashes at him while fixing a question on his eyes. Rob has hardly noticed this because he's concentrating on chewing a tough piece of calamari and watching the approach of a woman in her mid-twenties with a face and figure that would chip the paint off a

Mercedes Benz. She sits down beside Todd and wraps an arm around his shoulders. By the time Rob has retrieved his eyeballs from the ladies cleavage and put them back into their rightful sockets and his groin has settled somewhat, he seems pleased and displeased as Skyla sidles up to Todd. Sharon's brows bunch as she recoils into herself.

"This is Sharon and Rob, Skyla; this is Skyla, Sharon and Rob. She's my receptionist at the front desk."

Rob stands to take her hand. "Pleased to meet you Skyla."

She nods and Rob sits.

"Will you join us for steak a lobster in the restaurant, Skyla," Todd asks. "We'll be doing some dancing and we'll both need partners?"

"Does a cow go moo," she lilts in his ear.

A short time later, the four walk onto the deep red carpeting of the dining area. Crystal chandlers cast a mottled dim pattern across the candle lit tables while flickering flames caress the features of lovers as their lips caress the rims of their wine glasses and their eyes caress each others minds. In one corner, a trio, a sweet saxophone, a mellow guitar and a shuffling drum play a tasty improvisation of 'You Live in the Shadows of my Mind'.

The four sit as the waitress approaches. "I believe we'd all like the steak and lobster," Todd says, nodding around the table for agreement. They all nod. "And two litre bottles of my unusual wine on ice, please."

The waitress nods a pleasant, "yes sir",' and leaves.

"Sharon," Todd says. "This is my favourite song and I would like it *so* much if you'd dance it with me?"

Without hesitation she gets up and takes Todd's hand.

Maybe Rob doesn't care, or maybe he doesn't even notice, for his eyes are romping all over Skyla. "Would you like to dance, Skyla?"

"Do dogs go woof, woof, woof?"

Rob must believe that they *do*, or he doesn't give a damn, for he gets up quickly and takes her hand. As they dance, Skyla hangs herself on Rob like an expensive stole that Rob seems to think he can afford. While across the room, Todd holds Sharon closely too, not as fervently perhaps as the other two but very comfortably. They meld nicely into each other and seem contented with this existence as they hum quietly to the strains of the melody into each other's ears.

And so the evening carries on with the exchanging of partners in dance and the enjoying of the delectable meal. In the end, Todd calls for the hotel van to drive Sharon and Rob home, for both have been seduced by the sumptuous food and wine plus something else that cannot be clearly defined, as yet, at any rate.

It's the next day, Friday to be exact, when Todd seats himself in The Supreme Coffee Nook. This time he decides on a change: a cinnamon roll and coffee. He didn't need to come here this morning but he felt it would be a nice gesture to save this young lady a seat again today. He has his notebook, so as he bites into his cinnamon roll, he jots.

"Hi Todd, thanks again for the seat." She sits down and sips her coffee.

"Hi Sharon, so did you two enjoy it last night?"

"Oh yes, and thanks for the free food and beer and oh those whole lobsters were out of this world. I never can afford food like that. That was really kind and generous of you; ah, *sweet* of you." Sharon smiles crinkles at Todd. "I *loved* every minute of it."

"It appeared to me that Rob did too."

"Oh yes, the bugger coming on to Skyla like that, after all we've been dating for two years."

"What I think probably happened was that he got the false impression that you were coming on to me, but of course, you weren't, but he might have thought you were and so he came on to Skyla."

Sharon, who was about to bite into her bagel, holds it in waiting before her lips to stare at Todd. She twists her mouth to nibble on her lip and looks away for a second. Then looking at Todd again, she sets her bagel down and lifts her coffee. It has to wait a minute too. "You know, Todd, he might have thought that, he just might have."

"Maybe I should stop coming here. I don't want to mess up your life."

Sharon fixes her eyes on Todd's. "You could *never* mess up my life, Todd."

Todd sighs as they continue to gaze into each other. Several minutes pass before Todd says, "I certainly hope not."

"But why should *we* change our lives for him. He doesn't own me."

"Two years is a long time."

"Yes, I know, then all of a sudden life becomes much more complicated. Things change, things happen, you meet people and you don't know what to do. And you asked the other day if I was attached. And as you saw last night I am, but I was wondering about you, are you attached to that receptionist of yours in some intimate manner."

"No."

"No? She was crawling all over you. Don't you like women?"

Todd laughs. "Oh yes, very much so. You might just say that at this point in time, I'm between women…let me rephrase that, I don't have a lady friend right now."

"Well, what *did* she represent, an accessory to your business?"

"Oh she just hounds me and I ignore. If you're wondering if I've ever slept with her the answer is no."

She giggles over her coffee cup. "That's strange, I just don't get it. I think Rob was ready to jump over the table for her."

"Did his attitude bother you?"

"No, not really."

"Hmm, it should have."

"Why? I'm not the type who becomes envious if he looks at another woman,"

"Oh really, anyway, sure I love women, very passionately certain ones, but you see, I don't get off on dating a girl merely to have someone to go out with or sleep with."

"Oh really."

He picks up his coffee and takes a sip. "If they don't do something for me I…I guess I just get bored with them."

She crunches her eyes. "It still sounds strange; a lot of guys will go out with any girl just to get her in bed with them. Hmm, it sounds like you expect a lot from them."

"Strange, eh? Then maybe I should rephrase that statement too. It's just that if we don't have that certain…well, call it magic or …no I won't use the word 'karma', but that exchange of some special feeling, then I'm just not interested. Do you know what I'm trying to say?"

Sharon gazes at Todd beneath those long curled lashes and with her cup in both hands near her lips, she slides her tongue tip along its edge. Then glancing at her watch, she says. "Oh, gosh, I must run. We'll continue this conversation next time. I'll think about that. Toodle." The finger wave and she's gone.

Todd doesn't go to The Coffee Nook for coffee again until Monday. Again he's reading the newspaper as she sits down across from him. "Good morning Todd, I missed you not being here."

"Yes, I had several projects on the go. It seems I have less and less time these days to enjoy life. Have good weekend?"

"Oh, yes, had a great time, Rob and I played golf. I'm just learning but he's quite good. And you?"

"Oh, just a quiet time. Nothing worth mentioning."

Her lips are slightly puckered held constantly against the rim of her coffee cup as she sips sporadically and gazes continuously at Todd. He shakes the newspaper; it's more of a self-conscious release than to rid the paper of its wrinkles.

After a short while, she says, "I've been tossing what you said last week around in my head all weekend, especially when I was with Rob."

"Oh, what did I say?"

"About having to have a special feeling about a girl before you'll date them."

"Yes, now I remember."

"When I looked at him and thought about it, I didn't know if I *had* that kind of a feeling with Rob. You sound like you've experienced it. What kind of a feeling is it supposed to be?"

Todd chuckles lightly. "I don't know if it's *supposed* to be, but yes, I experienced the feeling with a girl a couple of years ago. I guess that's why I'm not satisfied with less now."

"Would you mind telling me about it?"

Todd pauses for a moment and nibbles on his lip as he gazes at Sharon. "I guess not. Well, it was when I was attending UBC. I was taking square dancing as a physical education course, and the first day, of course, in square dancing you change partners often, well I kept getting this girl in my arms each time she came around. She felt so good so near to me like no other girl I'd had in my arms before, a very special feeling, I don't know, it's hard to describe but it was a warmth that penetrated our, well maybe just my clothing, my skin right to my soul. So after the period ended, I asked her to go to the cafeteria with me for snack. She did, and we continued to do this after each weekly dance lesson but she had a boy friend and so it never went beyond that. Then one day she wasn't there and I never saw her again?"

"Hmm, how interesting, would you mind describing her?"

Todd fixes his eyes on Sharon's. "I guess not, well, I see her as clearly today as I did then. She was a nice looking girl, not beautiful but had very pleasant nicely proportioned features and a trim figure. She wasn't of rich parents for she wore medium priced clothing but she dressed herself immaculately. Her hair was long, light brown in colour and hung to her shoulders and she carried herself with an air of satisfied confidence, not egotistical by any means, but the way she posed herself when the music stopped, the way she would tilt her head coyly as her smile created tiny adorable wrinkles of crows-feet around her smiling deep blue eyes…it, it, oh shit."

He stops turns his head away and bites his lip.

She turns her head away to say, "Oh dear, I'm sorry I brought this up. Gosh it's time for me to run, see you next time, oh my." Fingers wave and she's gone. Todd sits staring at his thoughts a long time before he gets to his feet and leaves.

"It's exactly a week later, that Todd is sitting having a scone and coffee in The Coffee Nook, when she sits down infront of him. "Hi Todd, how are you doing?"

"Oh fine, and you?"

"Oh, so, so, anything exciting coming up in your life?"

He chuckles. "Well, if you can call going to a wine and cheese party Saturday night with some big-wigs exciting."

"Going alone or a date?"

"Alone, maybe." He chuckles lightly. "I told you how I am with girls that don't do that *something* that I tried to describe to you, but then I guess I should give a few tries. The receptionist at the hotel hinted that I take *her* so I've been kicking the idea around, and who knows, I just might."

Sharon leans forward and rests a hand on his arm. "I know someone who would like to go with you and I believe she might be a good match for you."

Todd smiles at Sharon. "I suppose that would be okay, but I don't care for blind dates, I'd have to meet her first."

"Maybe not, you see I have an identical twin. I don't know if you are familiar with identical twins but not only do they look identical but they also have the same personalities and the same tastes. I've been telling her about our conversations here and described your feelings and …well, I guess everything that I know about you. She thinks she'd really like to meet you."

Todd looks away then twists a few thoughts around with his lips; finally he fixes his eyes on Sharon's. "Identical twin, eh? Hmm, yes, apparently they are often virtually the same in every respect, uh huh, yes I think I'll accept your offer."

"Great, I'll tell her. What time on Saturday do you want to pick her up?"

"It begins at six. I'd like to pick her up at four-thirty, if it works for her."

"It will." Sharon hands Todd a card. "Shirl and I live with our folks at this address."

Todd looks at Sharon. "This is a really odd situation, Sharon."

"How do you mean?"

"It's like a blind date and yet if she's *that* similar to you, then it will seem to me that I'm dating you."

"Hmm, yes, I guess it will."

It's four-thirty Saturday when Todd goes to the address Sharon gave him. He rings the bell and a middle-aged woman opens the door.

"Hello, I'm here to pickup Shirl."

"Oh, you'd be Todd then." She turns and calls up the staircase. "Shirl, your date's here."

She has trotted halfway down the stairs by the time her mother's finished calling and left. She's wearing a white frilled blouse with a powder blue jacket and a full powder blue skirt. Her hair is done-up in tight braids with a slim tress draped down a cheek.

"So you're Shirl." Todd says, stepping close to her. "Wow, that dress and the way your hair's done-up, it really does something for you."

"I suppose that's a compliment. In case it is, thanks."

"Hmm, you're like Sharon, you don't seem to recognize compliments very well."

"Not when they come at you that way."

"Sharon said it kind of that way too, so how do you mean?"

"Well, the implications of what you said *could* mean that the way I'm dressed and my hair is done does something for me, in other words to improve what needed improving. Get the ambiguity of your remark?"

"Yes, I suppose it *could* be taken that way, but I certainly didn't *mean* it that way. Sometimes I find myself having to rephrase things I say. With Sharon I told her that I didn't want to date girls that didn't do something for me. Now that has an egotistical ring to it. So I rephrased it and said, it's just that if we don't have that certain magic or don't exchange some special feeling, then I'm just not interested."

"Yes, she told me about that special feeling you wanted from a girl." She extends a hand, which Todd takes. "And she tells me you're a really nice guy." She moves past Todd out the door. "Let's go, we can talk in your car."

She seems to be in a hurry to get going but maybe it's just that she's not used to him, actually Todd doesn't care why. He follows her out the walkway to his car.

Once they're seated inside, he gazes at her. She smiles. Yes the crows-feet are there; those long curled lashes; the quality; the poise. "Thanks, Todd."

He just leans forward on the wheel and gazes at her. "Pardon me for staring at you but I've never seen an identical twin before and the similarity is amazing. Sharon says that your personalities, likes and dislikes are the same too. It's like I already know you, and yet I don't, do I?"

There's a slight pause as she frowns at the question, then her eyes crinkle with a smile. "There's a lot you don't know about Sharon and so there's a lot you don't know about me."

"Meaning?"

"Well, you haven't dated Sharon and done things with her. You've just talked to her in a limited atmosphere."

"That's right but I think I know her personality fairly well."

She grins. "I think I'm going to *really* like you."

Todd grins back as he turns on the ignition.

The wine and cheese party is in the conference room of the Crescent Valley Hotel Complex. A smart looking young man in a bellhop uniform takes their jackets. They walk in. There are many middle-aged couples milling about, the men are dressed in suits and the ladies in evening dresses. Pausing before a couple they know or wish to talk to, they sip from wine glasses and speak with language embellished with gestures that they would never think of using anywhere else. There are tables with open bottles of vintage wine and platters of a wide variety of local and imported cheese.

She turns to Todd. "Oh my, I'm totally out of place here. They're wearing evening dresses."

"Only the women," Todd says with a chuckle. "Don't you worry honey, you look better than any of them."

"Oh gosh, Todd, that's a nice thing to say."

Todd slips his arm around her waist. "You had no problem recognizing *that* remark as a compliment."

"Yes, but that was easy to interpret."

"Come Shirl, we'll get drinks and sample the cheese."

Todd pours two glasses of wine and hands Shirl one. He lifts a piece of cheese from the platter with a toothpick supplied in a minute vase. "This Danish cheese is really good, depending on your taste, that is. Try it."

She parts her lips to nibble as Todd holds it for her. There's something about the way she works her lips that makes Todd want to bite into them.

"Mm, yes, I love it."

There's a tap on Todd's shoulder, he turns to face a tall bald man with thin lips and a no-nonsense mouth fringed with a grey moustache. "How's the expansion project going?"

"Well, there are considerable wrinkles to iron out but I see two months, no more than three."

"Oh good," Then turning to Todd's lady friend, his face breaks into a slight resemblance of a smile. "And tell me, who's your gorgeous lady friend, we don't see Todd with female companions often, miss."

"Shril meet Guy Howard, Guy this is Shirl."

Guy takes her hand lifts and kisses it. She shrinks back a step and looks to Todd for rescue.

"Don't mind Guy, he's perfectly harmless, Shirl"

"Todd here is a great boss and he's got a great business head as well as being a fine fellow. Hang onto him Shirl, he'll make you a fine husband." He gives a half bow and walks away.

"Oh my goodness, he gave you a great resume, but this is all too much for me. I don't belong here. I should go."

Todd takes the wine glass from her hand and sets his and hers down. "Come Shirl, I'm not in my element here either, we'll go someplace where we are."

As they drive from the hotel, she says, "I don't get it. You're his boss and you own that huge complex but you're too young to have built up such a business yourself."

"Yes."

"And how come you don't drive a big flashy car and live in a mansion in the ritzy part of town?"

"Inheritance is a marvelous thing. A rich uncle of mine passed away and had no children, so his fortune was divided among his nieces and nephews. As for the car and mansion, I was born to average income parents and material things don't mean that much to me. Oh sure, they're nice to have but I can do without them and still be happy."

"Yes, well I was raised a plain-Jane, but like you say, it *is* nice to have decent things. So where are we going?"

"There's a nice little pub overlooking the ocean. You can sit on the deck and watch the boats come in and out of the marina. It's more to my liking and I think it will be more to yours too."

Later as they sit overlooking the marina, she says. "I don't know exactly what to *make* of you, Todd."

"What seems to be the problem?"

"I thought you were just a nobody like me."

"You, Shirl, are *not* a nobody. In the short time I've known you, with the help of your sister of course, I find you to be a sweet vibrant person with natural class, and I could add a lot more adjectives to describe the wonderful things about you. We are all merely people and just because I inherited money should effect how we feel about each other. People should be measured, if that's what you're into doing, on integrity, unselfishness and honesty, not on position or wealth. You are a sweet and lovely lady and that's why I adore you"

"Oh my God, you're scaring me, it's our first date and you say you adore me."

"I'm just being honest with you. Can't I speak the truth?"

"Honest, honest," she mutters quietly as if digesting the concept.

"You haven't answered me."

She looks at Todd. "I…sure you can but…I can't move this fast, Todd, your in a different world and I'm pretty much mixed up, you'll have to be patient with me. This is difficult for me."

"Why?"

"Because, I have to get to know you and it's like you already know me."

"Yes, I guess it is. I should be more understanding."

It's later, at her door. "Do I rate a kiss on our first date?"

She smiles. "Do you ask a fish if you can catch it?"

"But are you sure you *want* to be caught?"

When she doesn't answer, he takes her in his arms and kisses her; her response tells him to say, "Mm, that was very nice, Shirl; are you free tomorrow?"

"Yes, what did you have in mind?"

Todd rests a hand on the doorjamb. "I've been working so much that I'd just like to have a little fun. We could go in the late morning, have lunch somewhere along the way and then the beach in the afternoon. I know a nice private spot on the beach where we could walk and beach comb and swim, throw and catch Frisbee, just have some kids fun."

"Yes, I like that, so why don't I bring a picnic lunch and we could eat amongst the driftwood." She laughs.

"Sure, that would be fun too."

"So should I bring a bathing suit?"

"Not if you want to skinny dip."

"Skinny dip on my second date? Oh no, no, I already told you, I have to move slowly. I'll wear it under my clothes."

Todd shakes a grin at her. "But it will be wet after our swim. You'll have to take it off to put your regular clothes on."

"No I won't. I'll bring a blanket to lie on while it dries."

"Chicken." He laughs. "So there'll be a blanket, eh? Say sweetie, that's good news."

"Good?"

"Yes, Good."

"Why is it good?"

"Because we're going to cuddle."

"We are?"

"Oh yes, you see cuddling is allowed on my second date."

"Hmm, I think I'll allow it on mine too."

They laugh together. Then she steps over and holding his head in both hands gently kneads a kiss into his lips that he won't have any trouble remembering tomorrow.

It's eleven o'clock Sunday morning when Todd knocks on her door. "Hi Shirl," he says, as she opens the door.

She's swearing cut-off jeans and a pink halter-top. "Hi sweetie."

"Your folks home?" he asks.

"No, they've gone to church."

"Sharon around?"

"No, she stayed at a friend's place for the weekend."

"Rob I imagine?"

"No, a girl friend. Why so many questions?"

"Just trying to make conversation."

Shirl gives Todd a questioning glance, "I'm wearing my bikini underneath."

"Oh a bikini, eh? You know, Shirl, if a girl insists on wearing something, I would prefer it to be a bikini. I'm very partial to them."

"Oh you, you'd really like to get me in bed with you, wouldn't you?"

"Well I can certainly think of worse scenarios."

"Is that all you guys can think of?"

"Oh no, sometimes I think of getting you out of bed, like on this blanket on the beach. What's the matter don't you like sex?"

"Love it but not on our second date. Slow down fella, we got lots of time. It's more exciting when you don't know when it will happen."

"Okay, I'll spring it on you."

"But not for a while yet."

"I'm just teasing you, Shirl, there are a lot of other things go into a fulfilling relationship. I'll slow down. Hmm, so if there's no one home then there's nothing stopping me from doing this. He steps in and closes the door and takes her in his arms and kisses her deeply and long. Oh sure, she kisses back; after all it's their second date.

"Oh my," Shirl says. "But maybe, we should be going to the beach."

They drive along Beach Drive to the end and turn off down a narrow road half grown over with salmonberry and baneberry bushes. The long grass between the wheels, whispers against the under carriage.

"Where the heck are you taking me, fella?"

"To an isolated beach; you have to go down cow paths like this to find an isolated beach these days."

They come to a heavy chain strung from two large tree trunks across the trail.

"It looks to me like you're not going any farther," she says. "How come it's locked off?"

"That's because it's privately owned "

"Well, we can't get through here then."

"Not a problem." Todd stops his car, gets out and unlocks a lock at one end. The chain falls to the ground. He drives the car though and locks the chain on behind them.

"How come you've got a key; did you get permission to use it?"

"I don't need permission, it's mine."

"Yours?"

"Yes, it's mine through my inheritance. I've been kicking the idea around of making it into a beach resort, much like the Crescent Valley complex but with a marina and golf course, the whole-nine-yards."

"Sounds costly."

"I can afford it."

"Oh wow, you're loaded, aren't you?"

"Don't let it influence our relationship. I'm just an organically grown country boy who's been thrown into this rat race. I may abscond, relinquish obligations anytime I find a girl willing to move to the country and live on a farm and raise chickens and children. Do you know of any such girl? We'd have plenty of money so it wouldn't be a hardship. We could pick up a real nice farm already developed."

"That sure sounded like a proposal, if I read it correctly. You're really pushing things and I know why."

"So why is it?"

"You've spent a dozen times or more visiting with Sharon in The Coffee Nook. It's almost as if you've dated her that many times, and of course, you danced with her a lot that night at the restaurant."

"So she told you about that too."

"Everything. And so you've fallen in love with Sharon, not me; I mean how *could* you; after all, it's only the second time we've *been* together? And so it's Sharon, not me that you want to make love to."

"But what's the difference, you look and act identical? I must be in love with you too."

"Only as you see the girl you fell in love with, Sharon, in me, and we're *not* the same person."

"Some where in that elusive concept there may be a fragment of logic, so I'll give you that. I'll wait an hour to allow myself to fall in love with you. Anyway, lets stop the bull-session and get out on the beautiful beach and enjoy."

They get out, pop the trunk and take out the picnic cooler and blanket. The two pause to gaze out at the sandy bay that curves around several kilometres of shoreline. It's isolated. Streaming through the tall evergreens that ride the ridge, the sun's rays cast a saw-tooth shadow across the sand; while the 'sweet, sweet, I'm so sweet' song of a yellow warbler filters through the density of salmon berry and ocean spray shrubbery that hugs the foot of the cliff. Out at the oceans edge, like little windup toys, Sanderlings scoot in and out with the constant shifting of the surf, while a group of Dunlins, flying in tight formation, wheel and dip and rise in an aerial-ballet flashing light and dark patterns like Venetian blinds.

"Isn't this really great, Todd? The isolation and being able to view natures beauty untouched by man."

"That's why I brought you here."

"What do you mean?"

"So I could view your beauty and leave it untouched by man."

"Damned you, Todd, you're not being fair. I'm trying hard to do this right and you keep pushing."

"I thought I was doing the opposite, I thought I was leaving you untouched and that was what you wanted."

"Bull shit, Todd, you're being ironic and you know damned well you are."

She begins undoing her halter-top. It falls to reveal a bikini bra. And then the shorts drop the bikini bottoms are exposed.

"Mm, nice, very nice," Todd says, but doesn't touch. Instead he tosses his shirt off and loosens his belt. From the corner of his eye, he sees her attention to the area that dropping of his jeans exposes, which is a pair of skin-tight men's bikini swim-shorts.

Todd glances up at her, a slight twist of her lips and she darts her eyes away from the area that had caught and held her attention.

He says, "Let's run to the water and dive in."

She turns to glare at Todd. "Damned you, you bastard, you wore those tight men's bikinis on purpose, didn't you?"

"It was *you* who suggested bikini swimming attire, I was completely willing to simply wear skinny dipping attire. Besides, you didn't need to look, especially so attentively."

"Oh shut up, let's swim."

And so she dashes off across the sand with Todd in pursuit. At the waters edge, she scampers in with Todd behind. When it's waist high, she dives in. Todd dives in behind her. When she surfaces, he comes up beside her but doesn't touch. They swim about for a while until they've had enough. "Let's run up to our blanket," she says.

When they get there Todd lies down on his back with hands behind his head and gazes out across the water. She looks at him and lies down close beside him. She leans her head up and runs her eyes up and down him. Then she lies back down.

"Beautiful day, eh, Shirl?"

"It's okay,"

"Just okay?"

"Yes, there's nothing wrong with it."

"Are you sure?"

Her voice takes on a touch of testiness. "Of course, I'm sure, why the hell would I say there's nothing wrong with it if there was?"

"That's what I'd like to know."

"Oh you would, would you?"

"Yes."

"What do you mean by *that* remark?"

"It wasn't a remark, it was an affirmative."

"The hell it was, it was loaded with irony and you know it."

"That simple little word? Level with me, there *is* something wrong, isn't there?"

She stares straight up at the sky and tells it. "What could *possibly* be wrong in this beautiful setting lying here on a blanket beside a guy that doesn't know the first thing about how to treat women?" She flings her arm out toward him but she stops it short.

Looking down at her arm lying limp between them, Todd notices a nasty little scar on her wrist. He says, "So what's wrong with the way I've treated you?"

Pulling her arm back, she says, "You flaunt yourself and arou…er, I don't know, kind of entice me and do nothing."

"What would you have me do?"

"This is what I mean, if you were half a man you'd know exactly what to do."

"Well, what *I* would do as healthy normal man would necessarily involve touching, a practise that you are shying away from."

"I certainly didn't mean no touching at all, I simply meant moderate touching."

"Oh great, I'm a whiz at moderate touching." Todd rolls over to her and reaches for her far shoulder and pulls her over to him. He kisses her deeply allowing his tongue to slip between her teeth. She partakes and even contributes some inventive tongue moves of her own, and so he rests a hand on her tummy, lets it circulate in slow little circles. Her hand performs a similar technique on his tummy. Todd would press forward with this close manoeuvre but for the fact that he is required to be moderate. He's aware that her hand, although still circling, is gradually doing so lower.

"No, no, Shirl, only moderate moves, for awhile, okay?"

She jumps to her feet, "You bastard, take me home." She walks over to some driftwood leaning her head on a snag and shaking in tears.

Todd walks over as close as he dares. "Seriously now, honey, are *you* being fair to me? You came here in a skimpy bikini and I only dressed in the same comparable bathing suit that a male would. You turned me on and shunned me and yet I can't do that to you? Can you say you're being fair?"

Still crying she says, "It's just that I wanted things to go slower and they were but when I saw you like that and how I feel about you, I just wanted to love you. But don't you see, the reason you're moving so fast is that you're in love with Sharon and feel you know her well enough to have sex with her. I'm not Sharon, I'm Shirl, and we hardly know each other."

"I guess you're right. I visualize you as the same person. Of course you need time. Look, I've got a good idea. Let's go to some place for a good meal and a few drinks. I'm not free until Wednesday night but if you'll let me date you, I promise to be more considerate and aware of your needs, okay love?"

"Sure."

It's Monday morning at The Coffee Nook when Sharon walks over to Todd leaning elbows on the table and staring into his coffee. She sets her tray down. "Hmm, a problem Todd?"

"Well, it's sort of a private matter."

"A bad business deal?"

"Oh no, well, you're Shirl's sister so I guess I can confide in you as long as you don't say a word to her, promise?"

"Oh sure, Todd, my lips are sealed."

"It's just that our date Sunday didn't go well at all."

"Will you dump her?"

"*Dump* her, that adorable sweetheart, I could never dump her. It's just that I can't seem to please her, I mean she acts like she really cares yet she's holding back."

"Do you know why?"

"Shirl says it's because I'm really in love with *you*, Sharon. What do you think?"

"I…that is…possible I suppose."

" She says it's the image of *you* that I see in her that I want to make love to, not her. But if I love *you,* and you two are identical, then I must love both of you."

"But we're not completely the same, there are subtle differences."

"I guess, but the odd thing is that she even said she loved me but then she says she hardly knows me. It doesn't add up. There's something fishy about this."

She pauses to stare at Todd, or at her thoughts, then says, "Oh my, hmm, well the problem as I see it, is that your approach is wrong."

"Wrong? It's worked for me for years."

"This is a different situation, Todd. Now here's a little advice, you'll have to slow down and be patient but watch for tell-tail signs when you're cuddling up, wait for her to show her feelings and desires and then feed them. Don't jump in there with a preset plan like you would jot down in your notepad. Women in love don't respond to plans, they respond to intuition. And so you must approach your love-making with that mind-set."

Todd shakes his head. "My God that's brilliant. I guess we men just don't have the woman-smarts to pick up on these feminine subtleties. But when you explain it, it makes sense. I think that's the exact problem. I blew it, didn't I?"

"Oh no, no, you didn't, ah…at least it doesn't sound to *me*, from what you've told me, that is, that you blew it. You might have goofed but you certainly didn't blow it. On your next date with her, you just have to be patient and play it right, clue in to her body language inferences, the subtle nuances."

"Good Thanks for the advice, I'll keep an eye open for them. Oh I must go now and thanks again."

It's Wednesday night and Todd and his girl friend have already had their supper and are having a beer in the pub, when Todd says, "Say Shirl, why don't we go up to my suite now and listen to my CDs and have a night cap?"

She tilts her head. "I suppose it would be okay, but I *do* have a job interview in the morning and I must be alert for it so I couldn't stay late."

"That's fine."

As they walk into the lobby, the receptionist looks up from her desk. "Oh hi, Todd. Oh say, you have a lady friend tonight. How come she out rates me?"

Todd laughs. "It's a long story."

"Hey, she looks familiar, isn't she that girl that was with that Rob fella at the pub that night a while back?"

"Her identical twin sister."

"Oh *sure* she is. That's a new line." Skyla laughs as the two disappear into the elevator.

As they ascend, his date turns to Todd. "I'm flattered that you turn down advances from Skysss…er, that girl for me, she's a real sex pot."

He laughs. "She *does* give that impression."

Moments later, he opens the door to his suite and they walk in.

"Oh my," she says. "You certainly wouldn't have a suite like *this* unless you owned the place." There's an entertainment centre across one wall; the eight-foot high definition TV, CD and DVD players, the whole-nine-yards, so to speak.

"Would you like something dreamy to listen to, Shirl? Why don't you pick something out while I get our drinks? What would you like?"

"G and T please."

Moments later they are leaning back listening to the soft subtle sounds of easy listening music. They have been sitting close together on the sofa listening to the music and talking and sipping G and Ts, when Todd moves right over and kisses her. She kisses back. He takes this to be one of the nuances that Sharon had spoken of and so he leans her back against the sofa for a little petting and she joins right in. This joining in move is obviously another nuance so on he goes. Well, as things progress the nuances begin snowballing and it takes all Todd's resources to cope with them, until finally the nuances becoming irrelevant to the task at hand and for the next half hour there's a great deal of tussling and milling around on that sofa. Finally they part and she says, "Oh my, I shouldn't have done that."

"What do you mean, you didn't start it; I did."

"Yes," she says, as she begins retrieving her clothing. "But I didn't stop it either, like it's only our third date and…oh my, I encouraged you, didn't I…I've never acted like *that* with a guy before. I'm sorry, I got carried away."

"You don't need to be sorry, you were great."

"I did, I mean, I was, oh my but I didn't know it could be like *that*."

Todd retrieves his shorts. "That's the way it's supposed to be."

She slips her panties on. "It is? I mean, it was, wasn't it?"

"Yes, it was."

She lifts her bra from the sofa. "That was really something…but things are moving too fast. I need time to think."

As she raises her bra to her bosom, Todd says, "Here, let me clip that on for you."

"Oh, thanks."

He kisses her neck and nibbles at her ear as he clips her bra for her.

"Oo, don't do that, I have to collect my thoughts, this is moving too fast for me."

"You don't like this?" He nibbles some more.

"Oo nice, but I should get home, I have to be fresh in the morning. I really must think about this."

A short while later, when the two are standing at her door, he says, "I have to go out of town tomorrow and I won't be back until late Saturday night. How about if we get together Sunday?"

"Oh sure, just phone me Sunday morning."

It's next morning in The Coffee Nook Todd's reading the newspaper when she sets her tray down. "Thanks for saving the seat for me, Todd."

Todd folds the paper and lays it down. "So you were out with Rob last night?"

"Well actually, no, he's been out of town for about a week, but we're going out tonight. He's taking me to that new high priced restaurant, Sergio's Spanish Dinning. Apparently, it's fantastic gourmet cuisine."

"Oh, sound's excellent."

"And how was your date with my sister?"

"Very, very nice." Todd bites into his cinnamon roll. Then he catches a glimpse of something and reaches for her right hand.

"What are you doing?"

He turns her hand over to expose a scare on her wrist. "I never noticed this before. This scar, how did it happen?"

"Oh that, I cut myself with a knife when I was young cutting watermelon."

"Careless girl; could have been very serious." Todd says. "I didn't make a date with Shirl last night until Sunday. I thought I was going to be going out of town on business but it was cancelled and so I'm free tonight. I'm going to call her up and take her out. That Sergio's place sounds great. I think she'd like going there."

"Oh she'll be out this evening, something about a job interview."

"Really," Todd says, "She said she had one this morning."

"She's really looking around for work."

Todd nods then takes another bite of his roll. "Strange though, she never asked *me* for a job." After he chews for quite awhile, he says, "Remember when I told you about that girl I knew several years ago and the feeling she gave me?"

"Oh yes, of course, of course."

Todd has finished chewing and picks up his coffee cup. "I suppose I shouldn't be telling *you* this, because I haven't mentioned it to Shirl but I'm so elated that I have to tell someone and since you're her identical twin I'm sure it will be okay."

She squints those tiny crows feet, like she does when she's curious. "Maybe."

"She gives me *that feeling,* and it was especially passionate last night. I'm absolutely smitten with that girl I made love to last night, your sister...*Shirl.*"

"Oh my."

"And," Todd leans his head across the table to about a foot from hers. "At supper time, I'm going to go over to her house and give her a big bouquet of red roses and an engagement ring and tell her I love her and want to marry her."

Todd leans back in his seat and smiles broadly.

"You are? Shouldn't you wait until you…you know, can take her out somewhere special, have dinner and then ask her?"

"You're absolutely right, why I could take her to Sergio's tonight and ask her there."

"Oh no, no, Todd, that wouldn't work at all. You see, you'd have to rush things so she can attend her interviews."

"I suppose so, I'll just have to hurry over and catch her before she leaves."

"But hold on now, it's only your third date and you know how she feels about you rushing things."

"I know but after the way she was last night, I just can't wait, and the way she responded last night, *well,* I don't believe she wants to wait any longer either. Now don't you think that's great?"

She sits back "Oh sure, of course it sounds great to *me,* but what if my *sister* doesn't love *you?*"

Todd laughs. "Doesn't love me, oh mercy me, what a question. Why the *passion* last night, that was inspired by true love, no doubt about it."

"Well maybe, but what if she was to turn you down for some reason or other?"

"Well, it would hurt, your darned rights it would hurt, but I've been through it before and if that happens I'll go right over to that receptionist at the hotel and offer her the roses and take her to Sergio's for supper, and who knows, I might even be stressed out enough to give her the ring."

"Oh, that would *not* be a rational move at *all.*"

"Actually, I'm not concerned, I'm certain Shirl loves me. Oh, gosh, I've got to get going, see you next time." Todd gets to his feet. He gives that little finger wave. "Toodle."

As Todd leaves, she stares at the spot where the little finger wave was. *Okay, so now he knows. Well, I suppose it's just as well.*

Todd, dressed in a suit and tie and carrying a bouquet of red roses, he may even have an engagement ring in his pocket, walks up to the front door of Sharon's place. *Okay, so there's only one girl. What happens inside this door should tell me if she loves me or this has all been some silly game of hers.* He knocks.

She opens the door. "Oh come in Todd, my sister will be down in a minute. Let's go into the dinning room to wait. She has a surprise for you."

Todd hesitates for he suddenly realizes that damned near anything would surprise him now.

She turns and says, "Come now, don't be afraid, you're among friends."

But he almost *is* afraid as he follows her into the dining room. A table's set on fine linen with sterling silver cutlery and bone china dishes, full wine glasses and lit candles.

"Your folks having company?"

She turns and takes the roses from his hand. "Oh don't be silly, Todd, can't you see it's set for two, this is your engagement dinner that my sister and I have gone to so much trouble to arrange. We explained the situation to our parents and they said they would spend the night at dad's sister's place." She walks over to the table and slips the roses into the vase of water waiting for them. "I'll be leaving on my date soon and you two will have the place to yourselves. Isn't that wonderful?"

Todd's not sure if it *is* wonderful. He feels like Rene Descartes; all he knows for sure is that he exists because he is able to think, even though not too clearly at this point in time.

It's the creaking on the high steps that turns Todd's head and raises his sight to see Shirl or Sharon, or who*ever* she is, slowly descend the staircase in a deep blue full-length evening gown, her long tresses shimmering past her shoulders and caressing her cleavage and a smile that crinkles those tiny crows feet about her deep blue eyes. She walks over to Todd. "Hi sweetheart, I accept your marriage proposal."

"But I haven't *asked* you yet."

"Well, since you've chosen to rush things, then so can I." She laughs lightly then places a hand behind his head to draw him near for a kiss and as the kiss progresses, her sister walks over to the dining room table and picks up the two glasses of wine. "Break it up," she says, as she hands a glass to each. "But wait until I pour myself one." She returns with a glass of wine and raises it to meet theirs. "Let's drink a toast to years of happiness for you two."

With all three glasses raised high, all right hand wrists are clearly visible: the scar on the presenter of the toast but none on the other. The three clink glasses and sip but the subtle exchange of glances leaves something floating in limbo. The two women take light sips and grin at each other, while Todd swills half of his down.

After she feels the toast she has offered is complete, she gives her sister a light peck on the cheek and turning to Todd, she gives him a, well...a kiss a trifle more enduring than one would expect from the sister to his future bride. "Well, I must leave you two now, that's Rob's car that just pulled up." She slips her jacket from the rack in the foyer and turning at the door, she smiles those tiny crows-feet at the two. "Good bye, you two and happy trails. I love you both."

Todd drains his glass as his sweetheart takes his arm. "Come on sweetie, let's enjoy our dinner and the evening and night. It's just you and I now."

Todd gazes at her while gathering his composure as well as his thoughts and anything else he can scrape up that may help him understand what the hell has happened these last couple of weeks. But he can see absolutely no reason why any of it should matter a damn, for she's a girl with very pleasantly proportioned features and a trim figure. Her hair's long, light brown in colour and hangs to her shoulders and she carries herself with an air of satisfied confidence, not egotistical by any means, but the way she poses herself as she moves to the table to pick up the bottle of wine, the way she tilts her head coyly as she fills his glass with wine, the way she fills his heart with love as she smiles those adorable wrinkles around her deep blue eyes...it...it just...Todd blurts out, "Oh shit, I love you, sweetheart." Some wine slops as he reaches his arms around her and presses a kiss into her lips.

She kisses back and they part. "And I love you too, Todd, with all my heart."

"Oh, I almost forgot." Todd reaches into his shirt pocket and takes out a little blue box, but before he hands it to her, he asks, "Will you marry me, sweetheart, whoever you are?"

"Of course, love."

She opens the box to a beautiful diamond ring. "Oh sweetheart, you shouldn't have spent so much."

"I can afford it."

It's next morning and the two are lying in bed snuggling closely.

She says, "You were great, sweetheart."

Todd kisses her cheek. "You were great too, honey."

Todd's quiet for a while as if he's still trying to analyze the whole fiasco. "You know, in spite of you and that other girl being identical, that other girl and I never really hit it off. It was as if there was something stuck between us."

"Of course, it was me, you were rightfully mine."

"What exactly do you mean by that?"

"You know, Todd, being an identical twin with the same tastes has often presented a problem between my sister and I. I remember one time when we were just children, she found this box lying beside the sidewalk and she opened it and there was this beautiful doll inside. When she brought it home and I saw it, I wanted it badly. Of course, we *both* wanted it, but *she* found it so it was rightfully hers. We shared it a little but I didn't feel right about it because it wasn't mine. And so I told her that I wouldn't play with it anymore because it was rightfully hers."

Todd wraps an arm around her and snuggles closer. "That was a very unselfish gesture, sweetheart."

"Strange as it may sound, my sister and I have always been happy to give up something for the other, because being identical twins, we share a very strong bond of love and unselfishness. Oh sure, we have a feeling of sadness too, and naturally, the more valued the possession the harder it is for both of us, yet at the same time, more pleasurable. I suppose that's difficult for you to understand, Todd."

"Yes it is, and so you think Shirl will be alright with this?"

"Yes, you could plainly see when she left last night, that she was as happy for me as I was happy for her when I gave up playing with her doll."

Todd shakes his head. "That's amazing really, but will I always have to check your wrist to be certain?"

Sharon laughs. "Not my wrist, but a much more apt area." She lowers the blankets. "I have this birth mark right here."

Todd chuckles. "Yes, last night and the night before, I *did* notice it but other matters held precedence."

Jared's Opus

Crescent Valley isn't a large town, but it isn't a small town either. If you sit on that bench with the park at your back for a half-hour each day and watch people pass by on the main street, you're not likely to see anyone you know. Jeff does this often on his lunch breaks; not because he wants to look at people he doesn't know but because he likes to relax and read the daily edition of The Crescent Valley Chronicle while munching on his mock chicken sandwich. On Sundays he takes his son Jared to the park to play tennis with him and Jared's friend Nick. Sometimes the two boys just want to play against each other. At such times, Jeff will sit on the bench and read a good book

It's been four years since Jared's mother left Jeff's marriage for another guy and although Jeff has tried to find a woman, he has trouble with it. It's not that he's not nice to them, but *that* seems to be the problem. Why he's seen so many guys, the macho confident kind who always own their own lives, do as they please and the women will flock after them. Jeff is nice to them but that doesn't seem to be what they want. Oh he knows he's not good looking but some of those guys aren't either. No matter, the women still adore them. And it's not that he can't fall in love with his lady friends, he's capable of falling in love with most any woman; that's not the problem, it's that they only want to be friends with him. They leave with these words that seem to be meant to cheer, 'We can still be friends'. To which he thinks but doesn't say, 'Hell we can; it's all or nothing'. Of course, that's the way love works, there's no middle road.

His lunch breaks, while sitting on the bench, are the most rewarding because of a certain passer by. Why Jeff has even named her, Pretty Woman.

Might better have named her Miss or Mrs. Unattainable because that's what she is. But there's no law against looking if you can remain incognito behind a newspaper. Invariably at twelve-twenty she performs her strut. Jeff has got so he recognizes her footsteps, that confident gait that women of great beauty possess, and invariably, he lowers the top edge of the newspaper so that he can see those shapely legs swish her long skirt while her calves, thighs and hips shape the returning cloth elegantly as it adheres to her stride. Of course, Jeff is in love with her although he knows fully well she is far beyond his attributes to attract and ability to attain. So he goes through this daily ritual gazing and dreaming.

This particular Sunday, Jeff's sitting and reading while Jared and Nick are playing tennis; he hears the familiar gait and looks up. Of course, without the benefit of the newspaper coverage, he has to hold the book high: a far from normal position for reading a book. She doesn't seem to notice, because like most women of great beauty, her line of sight is straight ahead. The boys have finished their tennis and are approaching Jeff from behind. "See you later," Nick says, and leaves for home. Jared sits down beside his father and watches his head turn to follow this woman's cheeky departure around the corner.

"Dad, why were you watching that woman so closely?"

"Oh, it's just that she goes by here at twelve-twenty weekdays when I'm sitting here reading the paper and eating lunch. I just thought it strange that she'd be walking by in the same direction on a Sunday."

"Hmm, I see, is that the only reason?"

Jeff looks at Jared. "Of course not. She's absolutely gorgeous; gorgeous woman strutting down the street, she's the kind, I'd really like to meet, eh son?"

Jared laughs. "How would you like to be married to her, eh dad?"

Jeff laughs. "Who wouldn't, eh?"

Jared punches his father's shoulder lightly. "Yes, we could use her around the house, eh dad?"

Jeff punches Jared back, lightly. "She'd go really good with our new furniture, eh?"

They do the fancy hand-slapping manoeuvre that baseball players do in the dugouts. Of course, they both know she's unattainable even if she *is* unattached, which is highly unlikely, why Jeff can't even hang on to homely women.

It's three o'clock on a sunny warm Monday afternoon, when Jared and his friend Nick leave the Crescent Valley Elementary School and stroll down to River Side Park to play tennis. They're pretty good players for ten year olds, but of course, Jeff, who's an excellent player, has taught them both the fundamentals and practiced with them.

Nick is bouncing a tennis ball on his racquet as he walks alone beside Jared. "So what are you going to do on the weekend?"

Jared kicks a paper coffee container off the sidewalk. "I don't know."

Nick misses the ball and it rolls off the sidewalk. He manages to rescue it just as it's about to roll down the embankment into the river.

"I told you before you're going to loose that ball if you keep doing that. You've lost two already and dad's getting fed up with buying us new ones. They cost money, you know."

"What are you worried about, your father's got lots of money. He owns a store."

"That's no reason to waste."

Nick steps back onto the sidewalk. "It's supposed to be good weather so mom and dad said our whole family will go to our lake cabin."

"Your sisters too?"

"Yeah, I said the whole family, didn't I?"

"Well, I like Janice okay but Natasha pesters me."

Nick laughs. "Yeah I know; that's just because she likes you."

"Well, it's a funny way of showing it."

"Would you like to come along, Jared, mom said it was okay if I brought a friend. We can have fun fishing and swimming."

The two wander down the path through the park toward the tennis courts. "I'd like to but then dad would be by himself."

"Dad was saying to mom the other day, I wonder why Jared's dad doesn't get a lady friend, he's been single too long. He said to mom, 'If we ever split up I'd get another lady friend in a hurry'. Then he laughed. He was just joking."

"It's awful."

"What's awful?"

"When your parents split up. You better hope it never happens with your parents."

"Hmm, I've just never thought of it ever happening, they seem to really like each other a lot, you know, the kissing thing and all that."

"What do you mean by all that?"

"You know, what parents do in bed."

"Oh, that. So how do you know?"

"I can hear them, their bedrooms right next to mine."

"Oh, really," Jared says, as they walk into the tennis courts. "Well, dad tries to find a woman but they never go out with him very long. I don't know why. He's really nice to them. I guess it's because he's not handsome or something."

It's after Nick and Jared tire of tennis and are walking back to the street, when Jared sees Pretty Woman. "Sorry Nick but I just remembered something I have to do now. I'll see you in school tomorrow."

Nick bounces the ball on his racquet. "What's the hurry?"

Jared doesn't take his eyes off the woman. "Oh, I just promised dad I'd meet him at the store."

Nick skips off down the street. "Okay, see you in school."

Jared glances both ways for traffic then crosses the street. He stays far enough behind her so she won't suspect he's following. She turns the corner with Jared ambling along behind glancing in store windows as if he is merely wandering about. Of course, she never looks back anyway but there are other people around that may get suspicious. She goes into a novelty store. Jared hesitates outside before he walks in. The store is like most other novelty stores with an open area of shelves containing a wide variety of ornaments, jewellery and perfumes. He looks around for Pretty Woman but she isn't in sight. Another lady stands behind the glass counter. "Can I help you?"

Jared focuses on the containers of perfume as if he's really looking for a gift. "I'm just looking."

"Are you looking for a gift for someone?'

"Yes but I'd just like to take my time and find exactly what I want."

"Fine, take your time."

There's a row of small porcelain ornaments; a rabbit, a pig and several other animals. Another shelf contains a group of miniature ladies in long full skirts and frilly hats holding fans in their hands. He doesn't know they're made of porcelain, he just knows they're pretty. There's a woman's voice, it's not the lady's behind the counter; it's pretty with a kind of rich smoothness that's difficult to describe. Jared can't make out what they're saying but one woman laughs. It sounds like the tinkling of the crystal wind chime on the deck of his home. He turns to see the other woman walk out the door of the shop. Pretty Woman is standing behind the counter; it's his first close up look at her. He smiles.

She smiles. "Hi guy, can I help you find something?"

"I'm looking for a gift," he says this in a voice he tries to make sound mature.

"Is it for your mother?"

"Oh no, she doesn't live with dad and I, she left us quite a long time ago and she lives a long ways away so I don't get to see her hardly at all. Actually, I'm looking for something for a man."

"Your father?"

Jared looks at Pretty Woman and smiles. "Why yes, exactly."

"Oh, I'm so sorry about the split of your parents," she says, with a tone of genuine concern. "It must be very difficult for you."

"Yes and dad too. It would be nice to have a woman around the house like my friend Nick does. Let's see, maybe some cologne for men. Is there any way I could smell some of them?"

"Why yes, we have these sample spray bottles." She walks over to the shelf, slips a bottle off and sprays her wrist, then holds it close for him to smell. Jared's thumb and index finger takes her palm. "Mm, that smells really nice."

"It's called Raw Hide."

"Sounds like a cowboy should wear it. But it does smell really nice. Dad might like that; he's a mighty fine man. Could I sample several others?"

"Why yes, here let me spray your wrist with this. It's called Lust."

"Hmm, sort of like mouldy bread. Wow, you have lovely long fingernails. I could use nails like that. How do you get them so long and thick? If I try to grow mine that long they just break when I'm playing ball or something."

"You *want yours long?*"

"Well, actually just on one hand. But how do you make them like that, hmm, all those pretty colours and that sparkly stuff on them, real pretty." He looks up at her. "So are you."

The woman's eyebrows snap up. "Oh, well, thank you, but aren't you a little young to be noticing women my age?"

"Oh, I'm sorry but it's just because I don't have a mom around the house. Dad and I could sure use a lady like you."

She can hardly hold back her laughter. "Use me?"

Jared frowns at his mistake. "Oh I didn't mean use you like a person would use a tool or something, I just meant you'd be nice to look at around the house and talk to and do things with."

"Anyway, I grow them long and reinforce then with false nails and apply acrylic to them."

"Who does them like that?"

"Well, I do women's nails like this right here in my store."

"Hmm, how much would it cost for me to have it done? It would be just one hand, and I wouldn't want the fancy stuff on them."

Her laughter tinkles. "But why just one hand?"

"Oh, I guess you were wondering if I was…you know, different. Oh no, it's because I play the classical guitar and need long nails on my right hand to pick the strings with, and like I said, mine keep breaking."

"I see, well I'll tell you what, I'll do your one hand for nothing."

"Oh, when?"

"When can you make it?"

"I get out of school at three. I could come here at three thirty any school day?"

"Hmm, well, it has to be a day when I have Annette here to look after customers." She walks behind the counter and looks at a calendar on the wall. "Let's see now, this is Tuesday. She comes in Friday afternoon. I can take you at that time on Friday. How's that?"

"That's great."

"And your name? I'll have to write it down."

"Jared."

"Fine Jared, I'll see you then."

The Pretty Woman watches him leave. "Hmm, strange, he never even mentioned the colognes again." She shakes her head as another customer enters the store.

It's Friday afternoon and Jared's whistling as he hop skips along the street toward the gift shop. As he enters, Annette's behind the counter text messaging.

"Is the prett…I mean is the other lady here today? She was supposed to do my nails?"

Annette tucks her cell phone in the pocket of her slacks. "Oh, yes, you're the young guy that she was telling me about. Yes, she does that in the back. Follow me."

Jared follows her through the chatter of the beaded door hanger. There's a little room to the right with a chair on either side of a narrow table with a cloth pad in the middle. A small snake-stemmed light with a shade shines down on it. Pretty Woman is sitting in a chair across the table. "Sit down on that chair and we'll begin."

"Is it going to hurt?"

"Oh goodness no."

"It's just that I get nervous in doctor's and dentist's offices and this looks and sort off smells like them…not really but in a way."

She tinkles laughter. "It's absolutely painless, Jared."

"Good, I'm not pain friendly. Oh you remembered my name."

"I had it written down but I would have remembered anyway. I don't have many customers your age or gender. Now hold you're right hand out on this padded surface." She looks up at Jared. "No, nails up please."

"Oh yes, of course. Mm, you have beautiful eyes."

"Why thank you, so do you."

"Thanks."

She takes his hand with in one hand and a nail file in the other and begins.

"Mm," Jared mutters.

She raises her head. "Pardon me?"

"Oh nothing." Of course, it was something, it was that marvelous soft woman touch that Jared has not felt since he last saw his mother. Now he's not thinking of himself so much as how his father would love this touch. Although his father plays the classical guitar too, his nails are thick and strong and he would never consent to having this done to his nails.

The woman lays the file down and picks up a thing shaped like a file but padded and buffs his nails. She leans forward into her work and her low cut blouse, which all women seem bent on wearing these days, reveals ample cleavage.

"Mm."

She glances up at him but says nothing as she again attends to her work.

"How long will they last?"

"Oh likely three to four weeks depending on how hard you are on them."

"I was thinking since we'll be seeing each other fairly often it would be nice if I knew your name."

"Oh, I'm sorry, it's Samantha, but people just call me Sam."

"Oh really, that's a man's name. I'll call you Samantha, it's pretty too."

She doesn't reply but smiles sweetly. *What do we have here a little Romeo? Cute.*

"Are you married?" Jared asks.

"No, why did you want to date me?"

"Oh no, no, you're too old for me, I was just wondering that's all."

"Well, I'm glad you noticed."

"Why haven't you married? You're sure pretty enough to get any man you wanted."

"Oh, thank you. Oh it's just that Mr. Right hasn't come along yet. Do you have any girl friends?"

"Well my friend Nick's sister pesters me and he says it's because she likes me but I get shy when I'm around girls my age. I don't know why. I guess I'm just like dad."

"Why don't you bring your guitar in on Monday after school and play it for me. I'd like to see how good these nails work. I could advertise for other guitar players to have theirs done."

"Oh, sure, I like playing for people. And I can play really well, but dad is a much better player. He can play all types of music really great and sings really well too. But he doesn't play or sing much since mom left."

"Maybe he's sad. Why doesn't he get another woman friend?"

"Oh he tries but he can't seem to keep them. He says they don't like him because he's not handsome and he's too nice to them. But he says he can't help it because he loves them so much. He says women like men that are macho and do their own thing and don't treat their lady friends nice but women hang all over them anyway."

Sam tinkles laughter loudly. "He told you all that?"

"Yes, lots of times."

"What's his occupation?"

"Oh he's got a university degree to teach literature but he quit teaching when mom left and bought a store. He works there."

"What kind of a store?"

"Oh it's that little corner store on the corner of Spruce and tenth, you know, The Wright Store."

"I've driven by. I've often wondered why it's called The Wright Store."

"It's because my dad *is* Mr. Wright."

Sam slowly raises her line of vision to meet Jared's that is fixed firmly on hers. For a moment they remain locked until Sam mutters, "Oh." Then lowering her sight, she attends to his nails.

The nail job's finished now and Sam follows Jared out of the room. Jared turns at the outside door. "I'll play for you Monday."

Sam waves. "That's great, Jared, be happy."

When he's gone, Annette turns to Sam. "What was *that* all about?"

Well, you knew why he was having his nails done. I asked him to play some music for me. I feel sorry for him with no mother."

Annett's one of these women whose arms and hands do as much talking as her lips. There's a lot of fluttering of fingers and waving of hands and self-touching, as if checking for a pack of cigarettes, but she doesn't smoke. "Did he tell you that?"

Sam wrinkles her tanned velvet brow. "You're not going to believe what all that little guy said to me."

"Oh, Sam, you shouldn't have said that, now you got me all tingly with excitement; tell me, tell me."

"He asked me if I was married."

Annette throws her hands in the air. "I knew it, another marriage proposal and again you turned it down, right?"

"No."

"You accepted?"

"No, he asked me why I hadn't married and I said because Mr. Right hasn't come along yet."

"Yes, yes, and?"

"I asked him why he wanted to know and he said because he and his father could sure use me."

Annette tweaks her mouth sideways. "Use you? So did he go into detail as to how they might use you?"

"His mother left four years ago and his father needs a wife."

"No mother, awe, the poor little guy. Well what the hells wrong with his old man?"

"He said his father tries but he can't keep them. He says it's because he's too nice to them and women hang all over men who are macho and do their own thing."

"It's true, I like it when I don't know where I stand with a guy, keeps me guessing, on my toes, it's exciting. And then just takes me when I least expect it."

"You know what Annette, you're a floozy." The two laugh.

Sam walks over to the perfume section picks up the spray bottle of Lust. "You'd like this guy I'm dating now, then."

"Yeah, that hunk Brad, let me know when you're through with him, as if I could get a guy with those physical attributes."

Sam sprays her wrist and lifts it to smell. "I asked Jared, what his father did for a living and he said he owned that little corner store at Spruce and tenth."

"Oh, yeah, The Wright Store, I often go by there but I've never gone in. I like to go to classy stores."

Sam picks up the bottle of Raw Hide and sprays it on her other wrist and lifts it to smell. "I asked him why they called it The Wright Store and you'll never guess what he said."

"Oh shattered nerves, tell me, tell me."

"Jared looked me straight in the eye and said, Mr. Wright."

"Oh my God, he didn't? At last, at last Samantha has found Mr. Right."

Sam laughs lightly. "Wouldn't it be great if is was true."

"The little guy's working overtime for his father. Did he tell you more about him?"

"Just that he has a university degree in literature and can play classical music on the guitar and, oh yes, that he isn't very good looking."

"Wouldn't you know it; a major flaw. But Sam, you started to say something about that handsome hunk you're dating now."

"Yes, he's the type Jared's father was saying women hang all over, he's taking me water skiing on the weekend at his cabin at the lake. I hate water and I'm scared of skiing. I'll be running the boat all weekend."

"And hanging all over his wet self when he lands."

"Wants to take me kayaking rapids, snow boarding and when we watch TV, it's those baseball players scratching their crotches and spitting."

"That's when you have to hang all over him. What's he like in bed. After all, that's what counts."

"He's exhausted from all his strenuous sports and it's a quickie and sleep."

"Quickie, oh, quickies are bad, bad. Dump him for another hunk; you get about a dozen date offers a day in here. You can pick and choose."

"These jocks use me like a sports car."

"You mean, like jump in and go like hell."

"Oh Annette, I mean, like a status symbol, for show."

"Oh my dear Sam, cry me a river, they're gorgeous. Okay, so they're not your type, so why don't you try Mr. Wright? You want someone who's nice, intelligent and you like classical music?"

"Oh sure, after four years of trying there's got to be something very wrong with the guy beside his looks."

"Yeah, your probably right. He probably can't get it up."

"Oh, Annette your mind is always in the gutter"

As Sam leaves for home, she doesn't take the usual route. Now this isn't a conscious decision; she's hardly aware that she's doing it for her mind's on this weekend's date; something she isn't at all looking forward to. Her route takes her along Cedar, up ninth, along Spruce, past tenth and right by the store on the corner. Maybe, she should drop in there sometime just to see what it's like inside.

It's Saturday and Sam's operating Brad's boat as he skims along behind jumping waves and spinning around backwards; all the tricks that it's possible to do on water skis. When he finally tires out, it's questionable who's the most drained, he or Sam. She docks the boat and gets out. "You can tie the freakin' tub up, Brad. I've had it up to here."

He glances at her as if he can't figure out what's bothering her. Sam marches up the cabin steps across the porch and into the cabin. Moments later she returns with a glass of wine. She leans back in one of the deck chairs and sips her wine.

Brad is busy hanging up his wet suit and other gear. He walks over and flops in a chair, "Whew that was a workout, would you get me a drink."

"No."

"What?"

"I said no; I *won't* get you a drink. I'm beat from running the boat and pulling rope and I hate water and I'm going home because you never do things I want to do and you're not even nice to me."

"Well, well, listen to her."

"Well it's true." Sam gets to her feet, tosses what's left of her drink across the deck and picks up her jacket

"Okay, okay, you choose what you want to do tomorrow and we'll go do it."

Sam faces Brad. "Okay, we'll go play tennis at River Side Park."

"A sissy sport and I don't play very well."

"I'm going home and if you want to see me tomorrow, meet me at the park at eleven. Other wise our relationship is zilch…kaput…over."

Sam is at the park at eleven. She hits a few balls up against the wall at the far end of the court just to get warmed up. She's an excellent tennis player and figures that Brad is too, but that he said he wasn't just so she'd think he was putting himself out for her. He really wanted to water ski again today. A half hour later he arrives.

It doesn't take long for Sam to realize that Brad's a good tennis player but not nearly her equal. She beats him every set by a wide margin. Oh sure, she could let up a bit but why not knock some ego out of this macho hunk.

Two courts over, there are two men playing. One is much better than the other and as Sam is about to serve, she pauses to watch a good volley. *That guy on the right is toying with that other guy. Wow, can he ever play this game great.*

"Are we going to play or are you going to stand there ogling," Brad yells.

Sam decides to really turn her game up a notch. It's only a matter of a few volleys before Brad says, "Lets go. I've had enough of this candy-ass sport."

"Go then, I'm not." She walks over to the bench on the next court and watches the two men play.

Brad leaves. "Some women don't know when they're lucky."

The two men notice her sitting watching them; what man wouldn't? They decide to turn their games up a notch for the benefit of this beauty. Since the one on the right is far superior, he smokes the other man until the vanquished is overcome with frustration and throws his racket striking a concrete post and flying in pieces. "Well, that's it for *me* today, I'm history." He picks up his gear and leaves.

Jeff goes over to where his gear is laying on the bench and sits down. Out of the corner of Jeff's eye, he can see the woman. She hasn't gotten up to leave and he thinks she's facing his way. Now Jeff would love to go over and invite this gorgeous woman to play some tennis but beautiful women make him terribly uncomfortable. He doesn't know why. Maybe it's the contrast between his looks and theirs or maybe they just look too good to be true. He can see that she gets to her feet and yes, she's moving his way. This is too good to be true but too terrifying. Why he'd like to run but his legs won't move. No they're not paralysed, it's just that something way back in those recesses of his mind says, *'sit'*. He does. She approaches so near that he must look up at her. First view close up of this woman's features sends his eyes darting away but the magnetism is too strong and they snap back.

She's first to speak. "Hi, I was noticing what a great tennis player you are. Would you care to play with me?"

His mind says, *I'd love to play with you,* but his voice can only manage a 'yes'.

"Great."

As she starts down the court, he says, "You can play this end, I'll go to the other end."

She turns and smiles. "How considerate, thank you."

Apparently they are evenly matched and so both turn on their best game.

It's about an hour later when, she says, "Say, fella, I've got to stop, you're too much for me. My but you're in great shape."

"You're in pretty good sh…you play great tennis."

Sam goes over to the bench, picks up her gear and starts for her car. "Thanks for the match, we'll have to play again sometime if we happen to meet here." And she walks off across the park

Jeff mumbles to himself. "Sure, sure, if we *happen* to meet. Oh sure, I *could* have arranged a time with her but why, to have a big disappointment?

One look at that handsome guy she was with shows the slim chance a guy with my looks would have; dream on, guy."

It's Monday afternoon and things are quiet at Sam's store. That is, until Annette walks into the store. "So how did your weekend water skiing with the gorgeous hunk go, Sam?"

"After a day of hard work on Saturday, I told him I was fed up with his sports and quickies. He finally agreed to play tennis on Sunday with me. I beat the pants off him."

Annette frowns at Sam. "My dear friend, that's when you should have hung all over him."

"So he said, 'Let's leave'. I said, 'I'm staying right here', and sat on the bench and watched two guys who were playing great tennis. Brad left in a huff."

"Can I have him, can I have him, if he come in looking for you, and he will?"

It's as if Sam doesn't even hear Annette. "This one guy, could he ever play great tennis, I've never seen anyone as good. So I asked if he would play with me."

Annette flutters her eyelids at the ceiling. "What a question for *you* to ask a man, I mean, like does a cow go moo?"

"So we played and it was great. I couldn't believe the shape he was in and such smooth coordination."

Annette gets that far away dreamy look in her eyes. "Yes, I like men with great shape too."

"No, I mean in great physical condition."

"That too."

"Get your mind out of the gutter for a change, Annette."

"So when are you going to see him again?"

"Probably never."

"Why, pray tell?"

"Well, he didn't act interested in me."

"I don't believe it, well in that case, he was either happily married or he was gay. Hmm, but unless…"

"Pardon?"

"Oh, I was just thinking for a change."

"Anyway, I may run into him again at the court and we could play some tennis."

"You know, Sam, you're not operating logically."

"How do you figure that?"

"Just the other day you said you attract guys who just want to get you in bed. Now there was one who obviously was looking for something else besides sex. Now these are the type you should be keeping an eye open for. You've let your beauty spoil you. You've never had to work at getting guys and so you've been getting just what's flung your way. *You* need to do the searching and when you run across a guy like this tennis player, show him your interests, your personality, your mind rather than just your body. Oh, I'm not saying he won't like that too."

Sam gazes at Annette in total amazement. "My dear friend, Annette, those are the first intelligent words I've ever heard you say."

"Why do I think that's an insult?"

"You're absolutely right, Annette, I've gotten lazy love wise. I'm going to do the looking from now on and showing guys my intelligence, tastes and personality."

There conversation ends as Jared enters with a backpack and a guitar case in his hand. "I've come to play for you Sam. I'll need a low stool of some kind."

"Oh, great, Jared. Come in the back." The door hanger beads click and clack as he follows Sam into the back room. She slides a low stool out from under a corner table. "Will this do?"

"Perfect, Samantha." Jared sets the guitar case on its back, snaps it open and lifts out a guitar. Of course, it's a classical guitar. He sets it so that the large curve of the body is between his knees and begins to play. His small fingers move fast and skilfully across the strings releasing a beautiful tremolo melody on the treble strings with a slower counter melody on the bass strings.

When he finishes Sam claps. "Oh Jared, that was absolutely beautiful."

Annette pokes her head through the beads. "Totally awesome."

Sam says, "It looked extremely difficult to me but you played it effortlessly. I recognise the composition. It's Recuerdos by Tarrega, right?"

"Yes, it is. So you're familiar with classical music?"

"Yes, I have several CDs, of Olivia Morris. I just love those beautiful Spanish classical compositions that she plays. My but you're an excellent guitar player and so young to be so good. Who taught you?"

"Dad did, you should hear him play guitar. He can play any style. He plays a lot of jazz on his electric guitar too. Do you like jazz?"

"Yes, I love it."

Jared plays several more compositions for Sam. She thanks him for his recital and they say their goodbyes and he leaves.

Again, as Sam drives home, for some unknown reason, she happens to drive along Spruce. *Hmm, I'm curious. I'm going to go in there.* She pulls up to the curb, gets out and crosses the street. She'll make out like she's going to buy something, but what? How about some tonic water? But as she enters the store, the corner of her eye catches a man behind the counter reading a book. Something familiar swings her to face him. "Oh my goodness, you're *him*."

Jeff blurts out, "I've always tried to be," before his mind has time to leave the page. A shocked stare drops the book to the countertop. His tongue, oiled by the mist of nervous energy that forms between them, says, "Yes, that's right, I played tennis with you yesterday."

This sudden burst of genuine cordiality from this man, alights Sam's features with a smile. "That's right, so you're Mr. Wright."

Jeff grins. "That's right, I'm Mr. Wright alright but how come you're right."

Sam chuckles. "I'm not right, you're Wright, right?"

Jeff chuckles. "We're both right, but how…"

Sam tinkles laughter. "Jared Wright's your son, right?"

Jeff laughs. "That's right."

An old lady trundles through between them. "You're right and you're right, Jared's right, everyone thinks their right theses days" She disappears out the door.

Sam and Jeff lock looks and break into a fit of laughter. Jeff leans against the back of the counter for support and Sam leans against the front, their heads only inches apart.

When they settle down, Sam says, "That's the best laugh I've had in years. It's really nice to meet someone with the same crazy sense of humour as I have."

"Same here," Jeff says. "I haven't had such a good laugh in a long, long time."

Sam leans forward with both hands on the counter. "The strange part about this is, I played tennis with you yesterday and didn't even *know* you were Mr. Wright."

"Is that right?" Jeff says.

They both sputter a bit more laughter. Still very close to each other a bit of Sam's sputter lands on Jeff's cheek. Tinkling laughter, Sam says, "Oh how slovenly of me, and *you*, being Mr. Wright, were able to contain your sputter. Sorry, let me wipe that sputter off." Sam glances around for some thing to wipe with. Jeff hands her a box of Kleenex that was sitting at the end of the counter. She slips one out and gently wipes his cheek. It's a soft touch as if it cares. "There, that looks right now." A smile and Sam takes Jeff's hand. "I'm Samantha, people just call me Sam."

Floating on her heart-catching smile, Jeff says, "Pleased to meet you, people call me Jeff." He grins. "Among other things. Ah, but they shouldn't spoil a beautiful name by shortening it, Samantha. I'll call you Samantha."

"You already have, and I won't spoil a beautiful name like Jeffery. I'll call you Jeffery."

"You already have."

A shared chuckle and Jeff says, "But I *still* don't know how you know my son."

Still interlocked, Sam gives Jeff's hand a squeeze and lets go. "I did his nails."

"So you're the one. He wouldn't tell me where he got them done."

"And…he brought his guitar and played for me after school today."

Jeff straightens up from his lean on the counter. "I asked him why he was taking his guitar to school, he said to play for his class but he never mentioned you, I wonder why?"

"Hmm, yes, and he played the most beautiful Spanish classical compositions and so superbly. I have CDs of Olivia Morris playing some of them but they're so difficult I couldn't believe your son at…what age is he?"

"Ten, eleven next month."

"Really, at ten playing so beautifully. He says you can play much better than him and you play jazz too. I love jazz "

Jeff scratches his shoulder and looks away, then back. "Well, I…he may be exaggerating, somewhat biased."

Sam shrugs. "I'd like to find out. Anyway, we'll have to play tennis again. Let's set a date this time, okay?"

"Yes, how about next Sunday."

"Are you busy this evening?"

Jeff shrugs. "Well, there's Jared and I promised him I'd take him to the park to play tennis but…"

"Well, does he have a friend who plays tennis? Maybe we could play some singles and then doubles with the young guys. I think that would be fun."

"It always is when I play with them but four players makes it even better. But do you mind that sort of thing?"

"With the young guys tagging along, not at all. I love children and they're old enough to play some fun tennis with for a while, but then you and I will want to play each other too. So how's seven sound."

Absorbing the velvet texture of her features and the sunshine in her deep blue eyes, Jeff mutters, "Beautiful…it sounds great."

That smile and Sam says, "Yes it does, goodbye, Jeffery, see you at seven."

"Goodbye, Samantha. Looking forward to tonight."

As her beauty disappears, the mist evaporates. *How on earth did I manage that? Damn it, I don't think I can handle a friendship with such a beautiful woman.*

By six thirty, Jeff, Jared and Nick are at the park and on the court warming up. Jeff sees Samantha coming toward them at the far edge of the park. He'd like to walk over to meet her but he decides not to. *For me to expect anything more than a friendship is ridiculous, so I won't push myself onto her like I've done in the past with women I wasn't suited to and made a damned fool of myself. But I could fall for her so easily if I let these tennis sessions continue. It's just going to hurt that much more when it's over. I won't make a date to do this again.*

As she approaches the court, Jeff says, "Hi, Samantha, nice of you to join us. The boys want to play a little singles by themselves. They say I'm too good for them. We can play doubles with them later, if it's all right with you."

"Sound's great to me, Jeffrey,"

Sam's wearing snug jean cut-offs and a T-shirt; this surprises Jeff because Sunday she was wearing what looked to be very expensive tennis outfit that had a short pleated skirt. She sets her shoulder bag, extra tennis racquet and can of tennis balls on the bench. Jeff watches her forward lean pull the cut-off taut across her butt. He glances over at the two boys, who were playing in the adjacent court. They've stopped to watch too, until they see Jeff look their way, then they resume their play.

Jeff bounces a ball nonchalantly on the court surface so that when Sam turns she will know he hasn't been watching her. Jeff says, "You can take the first serve if you want to Samantha, okay?"

"Okay."

They play hard for about a half hour before Sam stops. "Whew, I need a rest. Let's sit on the bench for a break and then play doubles with the boys."

"Sure," Jeff says and turns and sits. Sam strolls over and slips a water flask and a small towel from her shoulder bag. She hands Jeff the flask. "Like a drink of water?"

"Thanks, Samantha."

Sam wipes her forehead with the towel. "You're sure in great shape for a guy who works in a small store. I thought I was in good physical condition but you, wow!"

So they small talk for a while and then the boys come over wanting to play doubles. They do this until everyone is tuckered out.

"Well that was great fun," Jared says. "Did you enjoy it, Samantha?"

"Yes, Jared, I really did."

When they walk to their cars. Jeff's quiet. So is Sam, for a while.

"Did you enjoy the tennis, Jeffery?"

"Yes, Samantha, of course."

"You seem sort of quiet, I was just wondering. Do you still love her?"

Jeff flips his racket nervously. "Oh, so Jared told you all that too? Well, I don't know, how long does it take to get someone out of your heart?"

Sam swings her racket to and fro as they walk. "I guess I don't know."

Jeff holds his tight against his chest. "You say you guess, do you mean that you've never fallen in love?"

Sam flips her racket in the air and deftly catches it. "Oh I've thought I was in love, when I was young and love was such a novelty, you fell in love with love over and over, just many infatuations. Even now, and when I tire of them and dump them."

"Do you have trouble with that?"

"Dumping them? Of course I have trouble with it, it's never an easy thing to do if you're a woman with an ounce of compassion…but what else can a girl do, you can't lead them on forever."

"No, I guess not."

"And how about you Jeffery, how many times have *you* fallen in love?"

He's quiet for a while then he says, "Many, it's my nature. I love the girls but they don't love me. I guess I'm not like most men, when I fall for a woman I fall like a huge cedar, crash, and when it ends, and they always do, the same crash only the tree falls on me."

"Oh, that must really smart."

"Smart? It crushes."

"Oh, Jeffery, you're an *extremely* sensitive man."

When they arrive at their vehicles, Jeff opens the door of his SUV for the boys to toss their gear in the back. Then facing Sam, he says, "This has been really nice of you to be willing to play with the boys. Most women don't care for my baggage."

"Baggage, is that how you feel about them?"

"No, no, I love them both with all my heart, but it's how single women regard it."

"I'm single, Jeffery, and I love them too, don't judge all women by what you've experienced, we're all individuals." She turns and opens the door of her Corvette. Jared walks over to her. "Samantha, will you play tennis with us again tomorrow night, please, we love you, all of us do." Jared raises his eyebrows at his father.

Sam looks over at Jeff. "Is that alright with you, Jeffery?"

"Uh, …why yes, of course, I'd like that very much, Samantha. I'm sorry."

"It's okay Jeffery, don't fight it, let things happen naturally and be happy."

"I'll try, bye now."

"Bye." She waves and slips into her Corvette and drives off.

Jeff drives Nick home, Nick says, "Wow, she's a 'looker', how'd you snag *her*, Mr. Wright?"

Jeff laughs. "I haven't *snagged* her, Nick, she's just a friend."

"I hope you do. Jared here needs a mom."

"And dad needs a wife," Jared says.

"You're late," Annette says, next morning at Sam's shop. "It's eleven thirty, you were to be here at eleven."

"You'll never guess what I've done?"

Annette's arms wave about as if they have more joints than other people's do. "Oh my goodness Sam, don't do that to me. What? What?"

"On my way home yesterday, I stopped at that corner store and met Mr. Wright and you'll never guess who he is?"

"Oh, that's easy, he's Jared's father."

"But it turns out he's also the guy I was telling you about that I played tennis with."

"Really? It was meant to be. You've found your Mr. Right at last."

"It's too early yet. But Jeffery and I played tennis with Jared and Jared's friend."

Annette drums her long fingernails on the glass countertop. "And so, what kind of progress did you make with him, you know, the bed thing?"

"Annette is that all you can *think of?* You advised me to look for things other than the physical and to present my personality rather than my looks to a man. That's what I'm trying to do."

"I see, and how did it work?"

"Well give it a chance, we've only dated once."

"That's all it takes me."

"But you're a floozy. Anyway, he's a very sensitive man and I don't believe he's gotten his former wife out of his heart yet. We're playing again tonight, we'll see how it goes."

"Ah so he made another date with you, why am I not surprised."

"He didn't, Jared did."

"I *am* surprised." Annette dips her head endearingly to one side. It's her non-floozy side. "Ah, that sweet little guy, won't let you get away from his dad, it's so cute, so sweet."

"So is his father, if he'd only let himself go. At the store everything was great. He acted natural, we had a great laugh, he was fun and really nice, but then after we played tennis, he would slip into moods of gloom; I got my work cut out for me."

The next night they play tennis again, and as they did the first night, first singles and then doubles.

"Jeffery, you've done it again, you've out lasted me." Sam says. "You're in superb condition, how do you do it?"

"I play tennis a lot and jog every morning after Jared goes to school."

"You know, Jeffery, I've often wished I could go jogging, but you hear about these women getting attacked and I'm afraid to jog alone. I'd love it if you'd pick me up and take me jogging with you."

Jeff is looking down at his racket in his hands. "Sure."

"Your foreheads sweaty. Let me wipe it off for you, Jeffery." Sam puts a hand behind his head and wipes with the towel. It feels so nice. He glances over at the boys. Jared has stopped play and is watching Sam and Jeff.

"Come on Jared," Nick yells. "It's your serve." Jared turns to play.

Sam sits down close beside Jeff. He can feel her side against his. He feels that he should move away a little but it was her choice to sit close so… Jeff tries to talk but can't think of anything to say, it's this fear of beautiful women, well not fear exactly, it's more that he just feels he's out of his element in their company. Moreover, he has trouble taking his eyes off them but doesn't want them to feel he's staring at them, and on the other hand, doesn't want them to feel he's avoiding eye contact either. It's really a trying situation for him.

Jeff gets to his feet. "Let's play with the boys now."

Sam gives Jeff a questioning glance. "Sure, if that's what you want."

They play for a short while, then Jeff says, "We'd better get going Jared, you've got homework."

Sam and Jeff pick up their gear and head across the park, while Jared and Nick run on ahead.

"Something wrong, Jeffery," Sam says.

"Oh no."

Sam catches Jeff's shoulder to stop and turn him. Reaching into her handbag, she slips her card out and hands it to him. "Here's my card. It has my store and home phone numbers and addresses on it. Please come to my place tomorrow morning as soon as you're ready to jog. Will you promise to do that Jeffery, please, for me?"

As they continue to walk Jeff says, "Yes, Samantha of course I will, and I'm sorry for my…"

"It's okay, Jeffery, I think I understand, but like I told you yesterday, don't fight this, just let things happen naturally, okay?"

"Sure, Samantha and thanks."

"It's been a pleasure being with you. See you in the morning early."

"I can't go until I drive Jared to school at nine."

"That works for me, just drive by my place and pick me up then, at what? How about nine thirty?"

"Sure."

They're at their cars now and say their goodbyes.

Next morning, Jeff drops Jared off at school. He slips Sam's card out of his wallet. *662 Crescent Way, hmm, let's see, that street's off first street, the older part of town.* He pulls away from the curb. A short while later, he pulls up in front of her house. It's one of those old houses of the thirties: a cottage roof, gable windows and a veranda that runs across the front and one side. It's been well maintained with a hedge encircling and an apple tree and cherry tree in the front yard as well as a lilac beside the steps. Jeff ascends the steps and knocks. There a hustle of footsteps and Sam opens the door. She's in her housecoat.

Jeff meets her smile with his. *What a wonderful sight to wake up to. Dream on guy.* "Good morning, Samantha, did you sleep well?"

Sam frowns. "Good morning Jeffery, I know, I'm supposed to say yes, but to be perfectly honest I didn't. And how about you, Jeffery?"

"Not really either, but I'm fine. So what was *you're* problem?"

She steps aside to let him in. "Remember that guy you saw me playing tennis with the other day?"

"Oh sure."

She leads Jeff through the front room and into the kitchen. "He phoned me and wanted to make up, after our falling out at that tennis session."

Jeff steps back and bites his lip. *Oh, oh, she's going to tell me she can't go jogging with, etc, etc, etc.*

Sam pulls a chair out from the kitchen table. "Please sit down, Jeffery. So I had to take a sleeping pill to sleep and so I'm late. Like a coffee while I get dressed?"

"Yes thanks, Samantha." Sam slips a coffee mug from a rack beside the coffee percolator, fills it and takes it over to where Jeff is sitting. "I'll be back in a jiffy."

Jeff sits down. *Well, at least she's going jogging with me, or is she? Maybe, she's stalling to tell me she's back with that guy?*

A few minutes later Sam returns in the same outfit she wore to play tennis with Jeff. Jeff decides to make it easier for her to break the bad news to him. "So your boy friend doesn't mind you jogging with me?"

Sam, who's been pouring herself a coffee at the kitchen counter, turns abruptly. "Oh, Jeffery, *you're* my boy friend, *aren't you?*"

"Well, I…sure, it's just that… him phoning you and…"

"Oh Jeffery, I'd never do a thing like that to you."

"Oh, I'm sorry Samantha, I just…"

"Not to worry, Jeffery." Samantha walks over to the table and leans over and kisses Jeff on the lips. He'd like to get up and run, but her lips, warm, tender and caring, are just too much to resist. He kisses back.

Sam sits down and lifts her coffee mug. "Of course I'm your girl friend, Jeffery, I'm not the flighty type. And we'll go jogging after our coffee."

Jeff smiles at her. *Okay, so she's accepted me as her boy friend. I wonder if that means merely a friend or more? Why am I kidding myself, I'm not of her class. Hmm, but her kiss felt more like a lover's than merely a friend's.*

"You had no trouble finding my place?"

"I've lived here all my life and this is the older part of town so…" He looks around the room. "Hmm, I like these older style houses. They have more character, more interesting looking."

"Yes, I like them for the same reason," Sam says. "They're trying to copy this style with the long verandas on some of the new houses but it's not quite the same."

Jeff gazes around the room at the old but newly painted white cupboards and wainscot walls. "Yes, I can see your right. So you bought this place?"

"Oh no, it was my parents but they gave it to me when they moved back to Manitoba last year. That's where they were born and we've got a lot of relatives their age back there."

Sam holds her coffee mug in both hands and gazes over the rim at Jeff. "That boy of yours is a gem, Jeffery, he's so clever and really mature for his age."

"Not as mature as he *thinks* he is though. He can be a little rascal at times. Do you have any children, Samantha?"

"No, I've never been married and I'm not one of those who believes it's fine to have children out of wedlock."

Jeff smiles. "That's a fine quality but it seems odd to me that a woman… well, like you wouldn't have found a husband."

"Oh, I've found plenty of husbands, or they've found me, but I turned them down."

The two laugh.

"No Jeff, it's just that I've never met Mr rrr…I mean a man I've really cared for enough to marry. The one's that want to date me are the husbands and jocks and it's just for one reason."

Jeff coughs but says nothing.

Sam reaches across the table and touches Jeff's arm. "Jeffery, I was wondering if you'd teach me to play classical guitar sometime. I've always wanted to learn to play a musical instrument."

"Oh sure, yes, I could do that. But I'm really out of practise myself but…"

"Yes, but we could practise together."

"You'd want to do that with *me*?"

Sam gives Jeff's arm a light squeeze. "Jeffery, don't ever put yourself down, you don't need to take a back seat to anyone."

Jeff looks away. "It's just that I'm tired of losing. You don't know what it's like to lose all the time…every time."

"Yes, I guess I don't."

"Then let me *tell* you what it's like, I don't know what it's like for other men, but for me, when I see a woman who's opened herself to me but is no longer available, it's like death, a part of me dies, and I feel like I'm running out of parts."

"Oh my goodness, Jeffery, you feel things so intensely, relationships must be extremely difficult for you."

"The one's *I've* had have been."

"Why yes, Jared told me about you losing your wife, his mother and how you don't sing or play much anymore. But look at what you *haven't* lost at. You're skilled athletically, musically and intellectually. You've only lost at love?"

"But isn't love all that *really counts*?"

"Hmm, I guess your right, Mr. Wright."

It's Sam's heart-catching smile that brings a smile to Jeff's face.

"That's better, Jeffrey, smile more, and don't forget, *she* lost a great boy and you've won *his* love."

"Yes, I guess I should count my blessings. So the little guy told you all *that*, did he? He's so outspoken and…"

"He's great, a brilliant mind." Sam glances up at the clock on the wall. "Say, we better get going I have to be at my shop at eleven."

Jeff drives them to the jogging trail that runs along the beach and riverside. They have their jog.

"I'm sorry we had to rush this we could have stopped and talked more. You can run me home. I'll have to have a quick shower before I go to work. How about you?"

"I have someone at my store until one today."

"Tomorrow morning I'll get Annette to stay until noon so we won't need to hurry. You won't forget to pick me up, okay?"

"Sure, Samantha, I won't forget."

When Sam enters her store, Annette is standing behind the counter drumming her nails and gazing up at the clock on the wall. "Sorry Annette, but the reason I'm late is that I jogged with Jeffery this morning."

"All night jogging session, eh?"

"There you go again, Annette, that filthy mind of yours."

"There's nothing filthy about sex. It's a highly popular sport and economical because you already have the equipment."

Sam chuckles and shakes her head. "I just don't know about you, girlie."

Annette leans forward with that eager eyed stare. "So did ya do it, did ya do it?"

"Your advice to me was to show the guy my personality and interests. I don't want sex to cloud the issue. I won't encourage sleeping together until I've shown him my other attributes and we see if were compatible and love each other."

Annette flutters a hand full of fingers at Sam. "Hmm, you don't sound like you're merely thinking of this guy as a boy friend."

Slowly a puzzled frown creeps into Sam's flawless features. "You're right, I don't do I. But everything will be going along great and then he'll get quiet, it's like the calm before the storm."

Annette nods. "Ah, yes, still waters run deep."

"Hmm, I just don't know about him. And do you know what he told me?"

Annette rests a hand on the countertop and rattles her long fingernails on the glass surface. "Of course I do, I was a little mouse following you two around."

Sam goes over to the perfume samples and lifts the Raw Hide up and sprays her wrist. "He said he was tired of losing and that I didn't know what it was like to always lose."

Annette nods. "He's right, you don't. I don't believe you've ever lost at love."

"That's true and when I said I didn't know, he said, let me tell you what it's like, when I see a woman who's opened herself to me and is no longer available, it's like death, a part of me dies."

"Wow, this guy's profound, super sensitive, oh my goodness Sam, are you going to be able to deal with this guy?"

Sam lifts her wrist to smell the sweet scent. "His confidence is shattered, and I know he's afraid of getting too close in our relationship for fear of losing again. But he shouldn't lose. You can see the intelligence in the shadows of his eyes. And he's so warm and…just so…I don't know, just so nice."

"Shadows of his eyes, you say?" Annett shakes a frown at Sam. "Oh my goodness, Samantha, I hate to tell you this but you're in love with him already."

"Maybe I am, Annette, maybe I am, or is it just something different, a challenge."

"Shadows of his eyes?" Annette flutters her eyelids at the ceiling fan. "Give me a break, dear friend, it may be a challenge to hook him but it's love."

It's another one of those sunny spring mornings that finds Jeff and Sam trotting along the walkway along the river. As they approach a bench, Sam pulls up, "Let's take a break and enjoy the scenery."

"Sure." Jeff stops and gazes at the sparkling ripples of water. Sam sits down on the bench and Jeff sits about two feet from her. She slides over until her hips are touching his. She unhooks the water flask from her belt and unscrews the lid. "Like a drink of water, Jeffery?"

"Sure, thanks." He takes the flask and tips it to his lips and hands it back.

She slips an arm around his waste. "You seem to enjoy reading a lot. What kind of books do you read?"

"I prefer literary fiction."

"That would figure since you have a degree in literature and have taught it."

"What *didn't* that little rascal tell you?"

Sam gives Jeff a little squeeze. "I don't know what he missed out telling me but I hope to find out. But what exactly *is* literary fiction?"

Jeff turns to face Sam. "It's an art form. You see, there's a spectrum in fiction writing that runs from escape fiction to literary. Escape fiction is a craft written by a formula design to please the reader by giving him an escape from true reality."

"Such as?"

"Some of those romance and western novels."

Sam snuggles closer. "I see."

"Now literary fiction, on the other hand, deals truthfully with the aspects of human interaction, and most often, with the less pleasant aspects. But what makes it interesting to the careful reader, and I might add, perceptive reader, is there's often an underlying story or meaning which challenges the reader to interpret and when he does, and *if* he does, he feels a sense of being involved and clever enough to have interpreted it."

"You mean, get the gist of the story?"

"Yes, that's another way of putting it."

"Hmm, you must have some books at home."

Jeff chuckles lightly. "Oh yes, I have a small library in my den."

Tightening on his waste, she asks, "Would you show me it sometime; your library; your books. I think I'd like to learn how to read that kind of fiction but I imagine I'd need someone to teach me how to interpret."

"Why yes, like I said, it's a spectrum so you'd start with literary that's easier to interpret." Jeff looks away. "Of course, this single parent job of running Jared here and there and the store, it doesn't leave me a whole lot of time for..."

"Some evening soon instead of tennis; guitar lessons; your library; would you, Jeffery, please...soon?"

"I'll see what I can do."

And so the days go by this way, after tennis some evenings, jogging some mornings, but little else, Sam is becoming a little apprehensive about the

Samantha verses Jeffery standoff. It's on these thoughts that she is musing at the miniature coloured glass flowers through the countertop.

"Hi Sam," Annette says as she walks into Sam's shop. "How goes it?"

Sam looks up from her thoughts. "Oh, so, so, I guess."

"Say-hey-lady, tell me your problem, as if I didn't know."

"It's just my concern for Jeffery, and of course, Jared too, it's just that Jeffery is so slow warming up. We've played tennis and jogged and talked, but he's avoiding taking me to his house for guitar lessons. And I practically begged him to let me see his library of books but he keeps putting me off. He even shies away from kissing me. He's like a Van Gogh or a Picasso; he loves very deeply and intensely, and that quiet is like the calm before the storm, that's the part that worries me. What am I going to do, Annette, rescue me."

Annette gives a little sideways jig. "You know these geniuses, on the edge, eh?"

"No, no, he's not *that* bad but it's been about two weeks and it should be getting at least to the kissing and light petting stage."

Annette steps over to the counter and leans forward to whisper to Sam. "Don't let this out, Sam, but I get highly emotional at times too."

"It's common public knowledge, Annette."

The two laugh

"That's better, Sam, now let me dip into my wisdom pot and see what I come up with. First off, don't beg, don't ask; he's obviously the type you have to be the aggressor with."

"I wasn't aware that there was such a man."

"Oh yeah, Annette here has met them all, now what *you* have to do is take the initiative but be subtle about it. Don't scare him off. Now I want you to go to his store right away and lean over the counter put a hand behind his head pull it forward and kiss him long and deeply until he kisses back. No tongue stuff, just clean cut naïve boy and girl stuff. Got that?"

Sam chuckles. "Yes, I got that."

"Don't laugh, Sam, this is serious stuff. Next, tell him that you want to have the guitar lesson tonight at *his* house. Once that has sunken in, tell him you want keys to his house because you're going to cook supper for him, Jared and yourself. Don't ask him, tell him."

"A flaw in your plan already. I can't cook."

"You can't? How have you been eating?"

"TV dinners and takeouts."

"Why, Sam, you're not even blond. Not to worry, takeout Chinese food will work. Hide the containers in your car."

"What if he realizes that I bought supper and can't cook?"

"That's good, he'll begin to realize you're human and not to be feared."

"I can swing that." Sam laughs. "What next, oh wise one?"

"I don't need to go into detail, you know the rest, the wine and candles with supper, play dumb with the lesson so he comes close, wine and soft music after, then some petting to the point where he's getting aroused then say you have to get home early and go."

"Poor guy."

"Then tomorrow inform me of the results."

They both have a good laugh.

"Go now, Sam, I'll take care of things here."

A short time later, Sam steps inside the door of Jeff's store. "Hi, Jeffery, how are you doing?"

"Fine, Samantha, nice to see you. How are you doing?"

"Oh great." She steps over to the counter, reaches and pulls Jeff's head forward and applies that kiss, Annette referred to. He kisses back. A customer enters the store and they jump apart. The customer carries on into the aisle of canned meats.

"Jeffery, I you're going to give me a guitar lesson tonight at your house."

"I know I've been putting it off. This single parent thing routine keeps me busy."

"You're not putting it off any longer. Give me your house key. I'll go make supper for us and then you'll have time to give me a guitar lesson. After, we can relax with a glass of wine before I go home."

The words 'I go home' seem to relax Jeff. "Sounds great." Reaching under the counter, he lifts out a large ring marked 'house keys' and hands it to Sam. "Look Samantha, I know this must be difficult for you, but I'm having trouble with this for several reasons. I hope you don't get fed up and leave me, but I need to move slowly."

"Not a problem Jeffery, you're worth waiting for."

"You know something Samantha, you're a fantastic woman in every way."

"You're fantastic too, sweetie. See you at supper." Sam disappears out the door.

Jeff gazes at the empty doorway. *Loosen up, fella, give her a chance. Give yourself a chance. Keep this up and you will loose her.* Jeff is torn from his musing with Jared bounding through the door. "Hi, dad, what's new?"

"Good news Jared, Samantha's cooking supper for us at our house."

"Oh great, is she staying all night?"

"Now slow down, Jared, we don't have an extra room and I'm not…"

"Dad, you need to step it up a notch."

"I know, and I'm going to go a little farther tonight but no over night stuff yet."

Jared gives a big grin. "I'm going home then. It will be great to not go home to an empty house, won't it dad."

"Yes son, it sure will."

Sam stands on the sidewalk assessing Jeff's house. A large shopping bag hangs from one hand and a wine bag from the other. *Nice home, like the kind Jeffery and I were talking about at my place that first day we jogged: the long veranda, the gable windows. The style dates it as about four years old. That would be about the time his wife left him. Couldn't handle the memories his other house held of her? Hmm.*

She walks around to the back door, unlocks and walks in. The kitchen is one of those with an island in the centre with a wooden cutting block, an electric stove with pots and pans hanging done beside the range hood. Above the sink, a large window with flowered curtains centres walnut cupboards and beige patterned countertop. Inset in the lower section of the cupboards is the dishwasher and oven with the fridge off to one side. There's a small table in the kitchen area with just two chairs.

Hmm, for a two person family, sad, but I'll fix that. Nice kitchen. I must learn to cook. Small magnets with wise anecdotes on them; 'Women are like roses, watch out for their thorns'. Oh, oh, Jeff's hurting heart. And this one; 'All kids are gifted, some just open their packages sooner'; like Jared. Ah pictures of Jeff's precious possession, Jared playing soccer, swinging a golf club and offering the world a smiling face. Oh what's this note about? 'Dear Mr. Wright, as you know Jared is a straight A student even though he has been skipped a year ahead. We are aware that you believe he should be in a class with students close to his age.

However, he is finding the work too easy and needs to be challenged. We would like you to phone us so we can arrange a meeting to discuss skipping him again. Please contact us soon.' *Hmm, really, wow, what a boy!*

Sam sets the bags on the counter and takes the contents out. She opens the drawer below the oven, slips out several pans, spills the Chinese take-out food into them, slides them into the oven and turns it on to warm. *Who says I can't cook? Hmm, I'd love to snoop through the house but I want Jeffery to show me. Besides, it's not fair or nice.*

At the other end, offset in a large bay window area, are the dinning table and chairs. Nearby is a china-cabinet with fine dishes, cut glass and even candleholders with candles in them. She sets the table and lights the candles. Pulling out drawers, she eventually finds an opener, which with one quick wrist snap pops the cork off the bottle of Purple Mountain Shiraz. *It's going to take me a while learn where things are.*

Sam fills the glasses at the dinning table and takes hers to the little table. There's a newspaper lying there so she sits down to sip and read. *I don't know why housewives complain of the work, it's a piece of cake.*

Jared pops in the back door. "Hi Samantha, this is great coming home to a moth…a woman. What's for supper?"

"Chinese food."

He walks over to where Sam's sitting. "Oh, great, can I help you make it?"

She leans her face toward his. "Kiss please."

He grins and kisses Sam lightly. "This is great you being like a mother."

"I *will* be your mother soon, Jared, but about the supper; it's too late for you to held, the delicatessen already made it."

"Dad said you were going to make it."

"I was but then I thought I'd better not, you see, I can't cook."

"Gosh, what's dad going to say?"

"He'll be okay with it. It'll make him realize I'm human and not be afraid of me."

"Are you sure?"

"Yes, a wise woman told me so."

Jared goes to the fridge and opens it. "Speaking of wise people, I've come up with a wise plan to get you into bed with dad."

"Into *bed* with your dad?" Sam shakes her head. "At your age you shouldn't even be thinking about such things."

Jared takes a banana from the fridge, walks back to the table chomping on it with a smug grin. "But I have to, the way dad is, I mean I even had to pick you *out* for him."

"What exactly do mean by 'picked me *out* for him'?"

Jared pulls out a chair and sits down and in a tone that simulates wisdom, he says, "Well, it happened like this. Dad and I were sitting on that bench by the park and I noticed Dad watch you very closely as you walked by. You were obviously turning him on with that *walk* of yours."

"I have a special walk?"

Jared strips the peal back on the banana. "Oh yes you do, it's a very *special* walk."

Sam laughs. "You know, Jared, you're a little too mature for your age."

He grins and takes another bite of his banana.

"And so I turn your father on, oh good, I was beginning to wonder."

"Oh sure you do. He's often sat at that bench to eat lunch and read the news and every time that *I've* been with him, he's lowered the newspaper and turned his head to watch you walk by. He's really got the hots for you, Samantha. So anyway, getting back to my scheme; a day or so later, I was at the park with Nick and I saw you walking by and so I followed you into your store."

"Oh, so you weren't even *looking* for a gift."

"Oh yes I was, I was looking for a gift for dad, and I found it…I mean her, I mean *you*, Samantha." Jared grins. "Cool eh? Anyway, getting back to my dad gets Samantha in bed, or vice versa, scheme, I've already begun the next step. You see, there's an Olivia Morris concert at Victoria this weekend and I've already bought three front row tickets. They were selling them at the local music store. Now you have to help me book a double room and an adjoining single room. The concerts on Saturday, he'll want to go down on Friday afternoon, he always does when we go to Victoria so there's no rush. Dad doesn't like to rush things."

"Yes, I'm well aware of that. Now about these rooms, who's to sleep where?"

"Of course, we'll have to tell dad the single room is for you but…here's where we have to be crafty…after we get there and have supper, we'll take some beer up to the double room, and of course, we'll visit and watch TV. Now, dad always has to go to the bathroom after a couple of beers, so when he's in there, I'll slip your luggage out of the single room and mine in and go in and lock the door. The rest is in your hands."

"I see, and *what* is the rest of the plan, that little Mr. Mastermind has conjured up?"

"Isn't it obvious, you'll sleep with dad. Do you have a problem with that, Samantha?"

Sam chuckles quietly. "No, Jared, I think the world of your father and I don't have a problem with sleeping with him at all, but is it fair to spring this on him?"

"All's fair in love and war, besides someone has to light a fire under him."

"And I'm to light the fire?"

"Exactly."

Sam tinkles laughter. "Okay, precocious one, I'll follow your master plan and we'll hope for the best."

Jared touches Sam's arm and draws closer like all schemers do. "Trust me, it'll work; it has so far, with your cooperation, of course."

"And the wise woman."

A short while later, Jeff walks in the back door holding a bouquet of deep red roses and a smile. He walks straight over to where Sam is sitting and hands them to her. "For you, sweetheart."

"For me? Oh how thoughtful of you, honey," Sam says, then in a quiet voice, "Women are like roses, watch out for their thorns."

Jeff shades a frown at Sam, before brightening. "Oh yes, the little proverb on the fridge magnet. Just a weaker moment." He bends over and kisses her. Her hand slips around his head and holding it so he can't pull way until she lets him. When she does, he sniffs the delectable aroma floating about the kitchen. "What's for supper?"

"Chinese food, it's warming in the oven."

Jeff goes over and opens the oven door. "You didn't have time to cook all this."

"Who said *I* cooked it?"

"I thought that was your plan."

"It was, but as I was driving over here I had a premonition, I saw myself standing before your stove and not knowing what to do, so hastily I went to a delicatessen and bought take-out."

"Mm hmm, I see, so what *can* you do around the house?"

Sam leans an elbow on the table and rests her chin on its hand. "What a question to ask little old me, sweetheart, where's your bedroom?"

Jared, who has just carried Jeff's wine over from the dinning room table, snickers as he hands it to Jeff. "Here's your wine dad."

"Thanks guy." He gives Jared a light love punch on the shoulder. Then glancing at Jared, then Sam, then at Jared. "I get the feeling you two are ganging up on me."

Both nod.

Jeff sips his wine then chuckles. "Let's see now, I'm going to have to teach you to play the guitar, interpret literary fiction and cook."

"Yes, Jeffery, it looks like I'm going to have to be here a lot. Now about that note from Jared's teacher, how shall we handle that?"

"We?"

"Yes, I said we, I think you should phone the school in the morning and arrange for a meeting soon as possible."

With a firm stare at Sam, Jeff says, "You do?"

It's quiet, like that calm before the storm. Sam fidgets in her chair. *He looks very serious. Have I pushed him too far too fast?* "Look Jeff, I realize that Jared has been your only possession of mutual love, and you feel threatened by having to share that love with me, but you want a family, don't you?"

"Of course, I do."

"You probably feel you're losing a piece of that love but you're going to have me, Jeffery, and Jared's going to have me too. It's three against the world now, Jeffery, not just two."

Jeff looks away. "Of course it is, sorry, I've just *got* to get my head on straight."

Jared, who's been standing behind his father, takes his head in both hands and turns it to face Sam. "There you go dad, all straightened out and facing in the right direction. Carry on Samantha. How do you feel about me skipping?"

"How do *you* feel about it, Jared?"

Jared hangs his head. "Well, I've sort of been going along with what dad wants because he's been all I've had and I'm all *he's* had and…like no mother and so…" Jared's tone is near tears.

"Awe Jared, you poor little guy, but cheer up, you both have me now." Sam makes use of a soft hand against Jared's cheek and a face near tears to enhance these last words. "You will have a mother and your father will have a wife *soon*, won't you Jeff?"

Jeff's features, stern at first, slowly melt into a smile. "You guys, you're ganging up on me again, aren't you?"

The two nod smiles at him. "Okay, I'll lighten up and I'll phone. We'll all three of us will go to the meeting so we can discus it properly."

Jared had noticed Jeff's glass getting low on wine, so he carries the bottle over and fills, Samantha's first, then his father's.

Sam raises her glass to Jeff's. "Here's to the happy times ahead." They both take sizable swigs.

Jared feels the time has come to implement the next step of his plan, so laying a hand on his father's shoulder, he says, "I almost forgot to tell you, dad, there's a Olivia Morris concert at Victoria's Concert Theatre this weekend and I knew you'd like to see her perform. Samantha loves Olivia's guitar playing too, so, being kind of heart, I invited her too. Now I've already bought three tickets, they were selling them at the local music store. In addition, I've booked a double room for you and me and a single adjoining room for Samantha at the Snooze Easy Hotel. This arrangement will keep all three of us in close communication with each other, as it should be. The concerts on Saturday, so we should go down on Friday like you always like to do when we go to Victoria so you don't have to rush and can enjoy."

Jeff looks at the two each in turn carefully. *They look innocent enough and if I lighten up we could all have a real fun weekend as a family. What could be better?*

"Sounds great, it will be a lot of fun. Let's have some of that delicious smelling Chinese food."

Supper goes well and so it's time for the guitar lesson. The two move to the front room. Jared follows. Sam goes over to the sofa and sits down.

"Dad," Jared says. "Yes Jared?"

"We were right."

"What do you mean?"

"Pretty woman *does* look great with the furniture."

"Jared, your homework. Get to it."

As soon as Jared's gone, Sam asks, "What was *that* all about?"

"Oh, just a little joke between Jared and me."

"Oh no you don't, Jeffery, it was about me. Jared will tell me if you don't."

Jeff chuckles. "It's just that, Jared and I were sitting on that bench by the park and you walked by."

"Yes, he told me that you used to sit there every noon eating lunch and reading the newspaper and apparently observing my *walk*."

Jeff coughs. "Oh *sure* he would, the little motor mouth."

"But isn't his concern for you so touching. Where can you find love like that?"

"I know, I know, and I *do* appreciate it. He's all that's kept me sane. Ah well, anyway, Jared said you would look good with our furniture and I agreed."

Sam laughs. "You two guys. It's going to be great fun living with you two. I can hardly wait."

Jeff wants to get on with the guitar lesson. "Where's your guitar?"

"Oh I don't have one, I thought since both you and Jared play you'd have a few old guitars laying around the house."

"Well, we have several, their old but we never lay them around the house, they are far too valuable. I'll get mine and one for you."

Jeff leaves, returning moments later carrying two guitar cases. He lays one down on the sofa beside her and snaps it open.

"See I told you, you'd have an old one kicking around."

"Kicking around? Not *that* old guitar; it was made by Alphonzo Romero of Spain in 1885 and is worth a mint."

"It looks just like any other guitar, why so much?"

"Romero was a great maker of guitars due to, not only his skilled hand-craft but also in his selection of wood for their tops. A soft wood, spruce, with very fine and even grain is the choice because of its rich mellowing quality as it amplifies the vibration of the strings. And like violins, the ageing of the wood improves the tone."

"That is so fascinating. I've often wondered why the guitars on my classical CDs sounded so much prettier than the ones I've heard guys plunk on."

Jeff sits and takes it between his knees. His fingers move over the strings with smooth fluidity as he plays a beautifully melodic solo.

When he finishes, Sam says, "It's Tango in D Major the most beautiful melody I've ever heard?"

Jeff places his hands gently the guitar's body as if he's touching the skin of a beautiful woman. "To me it is. Such beautiful Spanish music was composed by the Spanish guitarists in the late eighteen hundreds."

"Yes beauties, and Jared played several for me at the store. He played them exquisitely."

"You sound like you're familiar with this kind of music."

"I've listened and read a lot of books on classical music and composers. But I've never learned to play it and that's why I want you to teach me. Oh how I'd love to play like you just did, to be able to make those splendid melodies myself. It must be a fantastic feeling."

"It is, but learning isn't easy. Finger-style guitar playing is probably the most difficult instrument to master, and you have to master it to play *this* kind of music."

"Oh, that sounds discouraging "

"Don't be, we'll start with easy solos and gradually work up. You'll be able to play tunes that will please you very soon. It's these compositions that Jared and *I* play that take years to develop the skill to master, unless of course, you're extremely gifted. I'll teach you to play them but you'll have to be patient for it requires hours of practice. You must enjoy practising or you'll never learn."

"How much practice."

"Three hours a day."

"I'll do it with your help, Jeffery. It'll be fun."

"Good, now for the operation." Jeff reaches into his guitar case and flips open the little guitar accessories box. He takes out fingernail clips. "Give me your hand."

"What are you doing with that weapon, Jeffery, I'm not nail-clip friendly."

"Cut your long fingernails off your left hand."

"What?"

"Short nails on your left hand, long on your right; a necessity for classical guitar."

"Oh the sacrifices one must make for love."

"That's true, the love of classical music has driven some men insane."

Sam clasps Jeff's hand. "I wasn't speaking of my love of music specifically. I would only make such a sacrifice for *you*, Jeffrey."

Jeff laughs. "Such is true love, here we go, pretty woman, it won't hurt a bit." He clips viciously.

"Yes it will."

"Oh how vain thou art, fair maiden." He chuckles maliciously as the nail clippings continue to fly.

"You're really getting off on destroying my beauty, aren't you?"

"Sweetheart, I cannot tell a lie; yes, immensely, I feel like a mischievous boy making a minuscule scratch on a Lincoln Continental."

"Wouldn't that be considered tragic to the owner? Jeffery, you're heartless."

He chuckles, "You'll thank me when you play your first tune."

Jeff hands Sam the guitar.

Of course, having watched Jeff and Jared play, she knows how to hold it properly. *Annette said to do everything wrong to get Jeffery close to me but if I do, he'll think I'm an airhead and can't learn.* Sam holds the guitar properly.

Jeff takes his guitar and fingers a C chord. "We'll begin with a few chords. This is how C chord is fingered. I'll move your fingers into this position… oh, you have it fingered already. Now the F chord, it's much more difficult to get sounding clearly. It's fingered like this, I'll…you have that looking correct but pick across the strings and let's see how it sounds…hmm, sounds perfect … now the G seventh chord…oh you have it too. Hmm." Jeff raises his eyes to Sam. "Have you not been telling me something?"

"I cannot tell a lie to my sweetheart. I took guitar lessons for a year when I was about twelve. But I stopped because being beautiful was more important to me as a teenybopper."

Jeff laughs. "Well, it will certainly speed things up but it'll hurt until you get those calluses built up on your fingertips."

After, Jeff shows Sam a few more chords and the C major scale, Sam says, "That's enough for me to absorb for the first lesson.."

Jared comes into the room. "Goodnight Samantha."

"Come Jared, I need a good night kiss please."

They kiss and off he goes.

Sam says, "I'll have to go buy a guitar and…"

"No, that guitar is now yours. "

"But Jeffery, you said it's worth a mint."

"Jared and I have a dozen different styles of guitars, we never play this one. It's yours now Samantha, baby it, no extreme temperature, keep in a dry place."

"Handle like a baby, eh?"

"Yes, and I was wondering, are you busy at lunch tomorrow?"

"Well, I don't need to be, I can have Annette look after things at the store. Why?"

Jeff reaches and touches Sam's arm lightly. "I'd like to have lunch with you, and since we're going to a concert in Victoria, I'd like to see you in something that really matches the occasion…why don't we go shop at that place that has expensive classy women's clothing, you'd look even more elegant in a beautiful evening dress. I'd be so proud of you, why I *am* so proud of you."

"Oh, Jeffery, you're going to spoil me."

"I hope to, Samantha. I hope to spoil you rotten." Jeff squeezes Sam's arm and chuckles. "And how could I not, you've spoiled me already, being so patient, being so…I don't have the words to describe you, Samantha."

"Don't then, let's sit and have another glass of wine before I go."

Jeff goes to the kitchen returning shortly with two glasses of wine and setting them on the coffee table. When he sits down beside Sam, she slips an arm around him. "You know, Jeffery, we need to practise becoming relaxed in each other's arms. Let's have a little smooch before I go."

And so they do, until Sam can feel Jeff beginning to squirm a little. "Gee, it's getting late and I *must* get ready for our trip to Victoria. Oh yes, and I *must* phone Annette tonight to ask her to replace me at the store at noon."

Sam gets to her feet and gives Jeff a goodnight kiss. But it's that *special walk* to the door, that over-the-shoulder glance with its suggestive lip twist and sly eye flutter that raises Jeff from the sofa and across the room. He takes Sam, oh, rather brusquely in his arms and gives her an enduring kiss. Eventually, Sam must pull away. "Now, really, Jeffery, enough, enough, I must go." She turns and opens the door. "Goodnight sweetie, see you at noon tomorrow."

Jeff says, "Goodnight sweetheart, see you then."

It's near noon the next day when Annette walks into Sam's store. "Hi Sam, soooo….how'd it…oh my goodness, what happen to your beautiful nails, didn't he like you digging them into his bare back?"

"Oh, Annette, you know we haven't reach that point yet."

"Was he getting ready?"

"In order to play classical guitar, it's necessary to have short nails on your left hand and medium length nails on your right."

"Hmm, I see, and did you get him horny then leave?"

"Did I *ever*, he almost attacked me with passion when I was about to leave. I almost suggested we go back to the sofa and finish the job but I was determined not to push things any further, besides Jared would have been broken hearted if his plan wasn't needed."

"Jared's plan is not needed? What plan? Tell me, tell me quick."

So Sam tells Annette of Jared's masterminded scheme from the time he noticed his father watching her walk by.

"Oh, isn't that darling, the little guy saw his daddy's tongue hanging out at this ladies sexy walk and…"

"I just walk like a normal woman does, what's different about it that would turn him on?"

"How could you walk normal, you're not a normal woman?"

"I'm not?"

"Oh dear no, now take a good look at me because you're looking at the most normal a woman can get and still remain a woman. Do you see guys following me in off the street?"

"Who's followed *me* in off the street other than Jared, and he's just a boy?"

"Brad, Luke, Dustin, Trevor, Harold, Rory…"

"Harold, who's Harold?"

"I don't know, I just thought I'd toss him in too, after all, he'll be around eventually anyway."

"I'd just like to know what's different about it."

"Oh my goodness, look over you shoulder, good friend, when you're walking away from a full length mirror sometime. But seriously, Sam, it's just so cute the way little Jared wanted a mom and a wife for his father and to pick out the one his father *really* wanted and to plan the whole scheme and carry it out, just darling, eh?"

"And clever."

"Yes, and so do you think you can swing your end of the plan in the hotel room?"

"Well, I'm sure Jeffery knows he won't lose me now, I've certainly made *that* clear enough, but I think my beauty scares him."

"Your description of his actions last night doesn't sound like he was scared."

Sam walks over to the shelf where the sample-bottle of Raw Hide waits expectantly. "I know, but it's been a long time since he's slept with *any* woman and it seems his last ventures were disasters."

"How do you know that?"

"I just put two and two together from things he and Jared have said. It's obvious the problem he's had."

"A problem, hmm, I wonder…"

"And, according to Jared, he's never gone out with a woman that was more than ordinary looking. You know, I think the idea of actually getting into bed with a beautiful woman scares him. Maybe, it's as if he thinks he needs to be a stud to please a woman of beauty."

"Ooo, don't you *ever* use *that name* in front of me again."

"What, stud?"

Annette vibrates her body with a head to toe shimmy. "Ooo, don't, don't, I get these oodles of goose bumps all over my body when I hear that name."

"Like I've said before, you're a floozy, Annette."

Sam sprays the Raw Hide cologne on her wrist and smells it.

"Why do you keep doing that?"

"What?"

"Spraying that particular cologne on your wrist."

"I do? Oh, I guess I do. I don't know. Anyway, we'll just have to wait and see what happens. It's like I said before, we'll be playing tennis and all of a sudden he'll want to quit and then he'll be quiet, it's like the calm before the storm, it worries me."

"So why do you want me to fill in for you today?"

"I'm going to have lunch with Jeffery, after which he's taking me to Charlene's Boutique to buy me an evening dress to wear to the concert."

Annette swings her hips back and forth. "Oh my, my, that expensive joint. Why your jocks never did anything like *that* for you. You got yourself a gem, Sam."

"I know and thanks for encouraging me. It's really helped me."

"Oh gee, dear friend, you're going to have me in tears."

As Jeff and Sam enter the boutique, they are confronted with a young plump lady who reeks of some obscure perfume. She may not have had a customer all day or she's new on the job, or both, for her voice assumes an affected lilt. "Oh you charming couple, can I be of assistance to help you choose something this grand day."

"Why yes," Jeff says, whisking a pink frilly blouse from a rack and holding to his front. "How would this look on me?"

Wrinkling her brow into a full-fledged frown, the girl sputters, "Well, I... that is...maybe if..."

"But is it really, *me*." Jeff asks, with a face steeped in concern. "That's what I'd like you to tell me, is it really *me*?"

"I...well...if..."

Sam takes Jeff's arm and gives him a pull. "Oh Jeffery, stop clowning. Pay no attention to him miss, he's just trying to be funny." Sam chuckles but the girl just stares at Jeff with an expression that seems to say, 'I don't get it.'

"To be serious," Jeff says, "We're looking for an evening gown for this lovely lady of mine. Could you show us a variety of what you have available? Price is not an issue."

"Oh, well, why yes, follow me." The girl leads the two through a maze of racks with ladies garments hanging like festoons of tinted lichens.

"Here's our top of the line evening gowns from three to six in price."

Jeff leans toward the girl. "Are we talking thousands here or higher."

"Oh mercy no, sir, hundreds."

"Whew, what a relief."

Sam is leafing through the rack. "Jeffery, stop teasing the girl and get serious." She slips out a powder blue gown with a full pleated skirt and holds it against her. "What do you think of this one, Jeffery?"

"No, no, no, Samantha, we want something that holds to your beautiful figure and shows it off, isn't that right miss?"

The girl nods fervently. "Oh yes, yes."

Jeff reaches into the thicket of dresses and slips out a deep red gown. Is this your size?"

Sam inspects the tag. "Yes, I think this might fit."

"Try in on then."

Sam scurries away to a change room. The girl goes behind the counter to fool with some papers and Jeff finds a stool just outside the change rooms. He waits. Later, he looks at his watch and continues to wait. This process is repeated until he asks himself. *How can it take a woman so long to slip on a dress? Why I could have put on a ski outfit several times during this wait.*

Eventually Sam walks out and stands facing Jeff. The dipping V trimmed with braided silver reveals her cleavage in all it's peach-like splendor. A sideways step opens the split of the skirt and out slips the smooth curved beauty of her leg. As she turns to face a full-length mirror, Jeff is forced to view a cerise satin sheen that hugs her haunch so tenaciously that he must look away. But not for long, for she turns and struts toward him, while looking back over her shoulder into the full-length mirror. *Oh, so that's what turns him on.* She pauses close to Jeff; well within his private space, winks then turns and struts back to the door of the change room. Resting a hand on the jam and a hand on a hip, she asks, "Well, Jeffery, what do you think?"

"Awesome, Samantha. It's yours." As Sam disappears into the change room, Jeff turns to the girl. "What do you think, miss?"

"A body and dress to die for," she mutters.

"But then what good would it do you?"

The girl stares bewilderment at Jeff. "What?"

It's late Friday afternoon by the time they reach Victoria. They're hungry and in a hurry to eat, somewhere, anywhere, how about that Taste Time Restaurant on the corner? Everyone agrees. Chicken potpies for all, a beer for Jeff and a glass of wine for Sam and they get to work on it. Later as the they drive off the restaurant parking lot, Jared says, "I guess you two would like something to drink in the hotel room, there's a *beer* and wine store right over there, *right Sam.*"

"Yes," Sam says, "Maybe some *beer* would be nice, Jeffery."

Jeff drives into a parking space in front of the beer and wine store. "Oh, you'd rather have beer than wine? I would have thought you'd prefer wine."

"I usually do but I've acquired a taste for beer hanging out with jocks."

Jeff touches her arm. "We can get some nice wine, if you'd like some."

"Thanks, Jeffery, but I'd prefer to have beer tonight, please."

"Exactly," mutters Jared.

Jeff turns to Jared in the back seat as he gets out. "What was that Jared?"

"Oh, nothing."

"We'll pick up some pop for you."

They watch Jeff enter the store. "So far so good," Jared says. "You handled your part just great, Sam."

"You're getting a real high out of this aren't you?"

"Yes, but we're not doing this for laughs, this is very important for all of us, we want to be a family, right?"

"Of course, Jared, but that was the easy part. In the hotel room, it's going to be tricky."

A short while later they are entering the hotel room. Jeff sets the six-pack of beer and can of pop on the desk and sits on the edge of the bed and stretches his arms out and yawns. "The drive was a bit tiring."

Sam sits in a chair beside the desk. "Yes the traffic is always heavy late Fridays over the Malahat."

Jared slips two cans out of the six-pack of Gold Stream Lager and snaps them open. "Dad likes drinking out of the can but how about you Samantha, would you like a glass, uh, a plastic?"

"Yes, and thank you very much for the prompt service."

Jared deftly strips the paper off one plastic glass and pours some beer in. The glass is too small to hold all of the can of beer so he hands both to Sam.

"Why thank you, Jared."

"Not at all." He hands his father the other can of beer.

"Thanks Jared, you're being excessively helpful tonight for some reason."

Jared gives him a questioning frown that seems to ask, 'Does he suspect?'

Jared sets the remaining beer in the small fridge beside the desk and flips on the TV and hands the clicker to Sam. "Since you're our guest, you choose the programs."

"A guest, well, thank you."

A half hour later, Jeff has finished his second beer, which had been pressed upon him by Jared, but makes no move toward the bathroom.

Sam has just finished her first.

"I'll get you another Sam," Jared says. He takes two cans of beer out of the fridge and snaps one handing it to Sam. Just as Jeff says, "I've had enou…" Jared snaps the other and hands it to him. "Uh, well, I guess I can handle one more."

This third beer does the trick, half way through it Jeff gets to his feet and walks into the bathroom and shuts the door. Quickly, Sam and Jared switch luggage. Jared slips into the single room. The door closes and the lock clicks shut. Moments later, Jeff comes out of the bathroom and glances around the room. "Where did Jared go?"

"Into the single room."

"Hmm, I guess he wants to watch something different on the TV in there until bedtime." Jeff mutters quietly as if simply thinking to himself. He looks at his watch. "Hmm, it's nine now, he should be getting ready for bed, but I don't like to chase you out of here so early. It would have been nice to have talked a while." Jeff sits down on the bed and picks up his remaining beer and looks at the TV screen.

"No," Sam says.

Jeff turns to face Sam quickly. "No what?"

"No Jeffery, he's locked the door and gone in there to sleep."

Jeff jumps to his feet, "Why that little rascal, I should have known he'd pull something like this. I'll phone the desk and have them come up with their master key." He reaches for the phone and begins to dial.

"Jeffery, " Sam says.

Jeff stops dialling and stares at Sam. "Yes?"

"Put the phone down."

For a moment, Jeff stares at Sam with the phone in limbo, then very slowly, with his eyes still fixed firmly on Sam's, the phone is lowered onto the desktop.

"It was *his* plan from the start. He masterminded the whole scenario and had a ball doing it. Let him have his fun, Jeffery, and let us have *our* fun."

Jeff eases himself back onto the edge of the bed. "Well, I don't know...Samantha..."

"Don't you want to sleep with me, Jeffery?"

"Oh my God, Samantha, there's nothing in this world I'd rather do but it's been two years since I've slept with a woman, and frankly, Sam, your beauty scares the hell out of me."

"Jeffery, I'm just another woman." She gets up and goes over and sits on the edge of the bed beside him. "I don't bite. I've had a lot of experience and encountered every kind of man problem. Just let me get things going and relax and enjoy. It's like riding a bicycle, you never forget, it will all come back to you in a flash. I assure you, you'll be great." Sam begins to unbutton his shirt. "You can start undressing me too."

It's the knocking on the door of the single room that awakens them. Jeff lifts his head from his pillow and looks at Sam. With her head still on her pillow facing him, she smiles. "I told you so."

Jeff smiles at her. "You were great. Samantha."

"So were you, Jeffery."

The knock continues. "Can I come in?"

"Give us a minute to get our robes on," says Sam.

The two get out of bed and slip their housecoats on. "Okay, you can come in now."

Jared walks in slowly with a grin on his face. He sits in the chair by the desk and shines his grin from one to the other. "Good morning."

Sam smiles at him. "Good morning."

Jeff turns on the coffee percolator. "Good morning." Then he turns and looks at Jared. "Why all the grinning."

"Oh nothing." Jared continues to sit and grin at them.

Sam chuckles. "I suspect it's more than nothing. What time did you go to sleep last night?"

"As soon as I went in the room I went straight to bed and fell asleep."

Sam's lying in her housecoat on the bed propped up with pillows. One hand is holding an elbow, while the other hand holds her chin. "Hmm, it was about ten when we heard your shower going, right Jeffery?"

Jeff lies down beside Sam and slips an arm around her neck. "Yes."

Jared flips a hand to one side. "Oh yes, yes, I forgot, as soon as I had a shower I went straight to bed."

"You probably did, but I was wondering what you did the hour before your shower."

Jared gets to his feet and paces back and forth while sneaking glances at Sam then Jeff. "Well, lets see now, the hour before, I was watching TV with you guys, That's when dad went to the bathroom and we implemented my master plan."

"What time was it then?"

"Like I said, ten bells."

"What program had just come on the TV?"

"Let's see now, oh yes, it was the Simpsons."

"Which starts at nine."

Jared stares at Sam, who fixes a stern expression on him.

Jared looks away. He knows she's right. He knows he has no viable excuse. He knows they know he was listening to hear if his master plan was a success and he was well pleased when he heard it was. But he says nothing. Everything's been said that needs to be said except. "Jared," Jeff says. "No more eaves dropping, do you understand?"

Jared splays his fingers on the desktop while standing on one leg with the other crossing over, a stance that signifies pride in mission accomplished. He says, in a mature voice, "Why yes, I get the picture crystal clear, but you'd think a particular person would be more grateful to the person who masterminded his love life into a viable relationship."

The two on the bed clap and cheer. "Bravo, bravo."

Sam chuckles. "Don't I get any credit?"

"Sure, you added the final touches very nicely, thanks for your assistance."

"Believe me, fellow schemer, it was indeed a pleasure."

As Jeff and Sam get caught up in an extended kiss, Jared informs them. "Enough of that, it's time for strawberries and whip cream on pancakes at The Taste Time Restaurant."

It's early Saturday afternoon, and after a morning of traipsing through the Victoria Museum, Beacon Hill Park and Butchard Gardens, these three return to their hotel rooms ready for some relaxation.

It's Jared who speaks first. "I don't have any idea of how you two may desire to pass the remainder of this afternoon, As for *me*, I'm about to go to my room to watch baseball, and possibly have a nap." Jared looks at his watch. "It is now two bells, I shall not come out of my room until five bells, which will be close to supper time. The concert isn't until eight and lies close by so that should leave us plenty of time to eat and get there. Now this arrangement is designed primarily to furnish you two with ample time to…ah…take a nap, well I'm not at *all* suggesting you merely *nap*, there *are* friendly oriented pastimes that couples often wish to purs…"

"Jared, cool it," Jeff says. "We get the point and thanks, but no eaves dropping."

Sam walks over and lays her hands on Jared's shoulders. "Thanks Jared, you're a dear, kiss please." They kiss and Jared turns and closes his door on a grin.

Then Samantha turns to Jeff. "That was so considerate of Jared to give us this free time. How on earth shall we make use of it?"

"How about the friendly oriented pastimes that he implied existed?"

"How would *he* know about them?"

"Kids these days seem to know everything."

"Are you familiar with any of them?"

Jeff reaches around Sam's back. 'zip.' Her dress falls to the floor.

"What on earth are you up to, Jeffery?"

"Friendly oriented pastime step one."

"Step two," Sam says, running fingers down Jeff's shirt freeing the buttons; his shirt falls.

"Step three," Jeff says. One quick finger flip sends her bra floating down.

"Step four." Sam bites her lips giving an almost vicious jerk of his belt. His pants fall to the floor.

Jeff starts laughing. "You know what this reminds me of."

"Step five, Jeffery, step *five*."

"An old twenties movie in which these two comedians took turns dismantling an old car by ripping off part by part until in was just a pile of junk on the ground." He begins chuckling then it escalates into all out laughter.

Sam stands biting her lip with fists on hips staring at Jeff.

When his mirth settles he says, "You and I have a crazy sense of humour, an intelligent person wouldn't be laughing at such foolishness, but it's just one of those situations where it's the mood you're in and little things just…"

"I'm not laughing, Jeffery, I want *step five now*."

"Oh yes, coming right up, honey."

"Good."

It seems the remainder of the steps unfolded without mishaps, for at five bells all three are dressed and ready to go to supper and look well pleased with themselves.

It's seven forty-five when the three from Crescent Valley walk into the Victoria Concert Theatre. Many couples mill about, some seemed bent on sipping status from wine glasses, others seem bent on clinging to the secure means of older men, others wander aimlessly as if bent on searching for a lost fugue, while others seem bent on tugging their parents back into the comfort of their beloved domestic banality. Others, like the Wrights, secure a program immediately and walk right through the lobby and down the aisle to their seats. Jeff and Jared shed their jackets and Sam sheds her knit shawl and they all wiggle into their front row seats for an enjoyable evening of great music.

On stage, there are two leather seats placed side by side with medium high backs and low arms offering the comfort and facility for playing guitar on stage for a whole evening. Several microphones on stems are placed strategically to catch the full tone of a guitar yet not be an obstruction. A guitar is leaning up in its stand like a lady-in-waiting.

At eight sharp, Olivia Morris walks onto stage from the left wing, smiles to the welcoming applause of the audience and very sedately sits herself in one of the seats, slips her guitar from its stand and places it in her lap. "My first selection is one I often warm up with, because of its simplistic beauty and popularity. Romanza Espanosa, in English, Spanish Romance. Who composed it? No one knows."

Her agile fingers play the haunting melody that floats on a triplet finger roll and deep bass. She repeats the melody with a tremolo that streams from the strings with the warmth of a summer breeze. As the solo ends she raises her fingers from the strings and nods to the applause, a polite gesture in appreciation of the response of the audience.

When the applause subsides, she says, "I suppose some of you are wondering why I have this extra chair here beside me. Quite often when I begin my concerts, if I see a child intently watching my fingers as I play, I like to call them up to chat and ask if there's a certain composition they would like to hear me play. I see such a child now. What's your name young fella?"

"My names, Jared, Olivia; I'm pleased to meet you."

"I'm pleased to meet you too, Jared, would you please come up and sit with me?"

Jared doesn't need any prompting; he's on his feet and up the steps in a hurry. He sits in the seat next to Olivia. She shakes his hand. "So how old are you?"

"I'm ten years old, Olivia, and how old are you?"

There's a tittering surfacing here and there in the audience.

Olivia smiles. "Well, Jared, that's a question women shy away from answering."

"Oh I'm sorry, I wasn't aware that they had a problem with that."

"Are those your parents you were sitting beside?"

"Why yes, they are. That pretty lady is my new mom that I picked out for dad."

The audience laughs with Olivia. "You picked her out for your dad? Oh really, what's her name?"

"Samantha."

"Samantha, would you mind stepping up onto the stage to show the audience the woman that Jared picked out for his father?"

Sam is hesitant until Jeff whispers in her ear, "Go ahead, for Jared, this is fun."

Sam gets to her feet and struts *that walk* up the steps and deep into the stage allowing the stage lights to glisten the cerise satin sheen of her strut. Pivoting, she struts back like an experienced model, pausing in the foot lights to present a heart-warming smile and finger wave. The crowd cheers as she walks back down the steps to her seat.

"Didn't I do a great job of picking her out for my dad, Olivia?"

"You certainly did." She laughs lightly. "Do you play the guitar?"

"Oh yes, quite nicely."

Loud enough for all to hear, Sam says, "He's a fantastic guitar player."

"Oh really, would you like to play something for us?"

"Sure if I had a guitar."

She places her guitar carefully in his lap. Without hesitation, he says, "I will play Recuerdos de la Alhambra." Feeding on the presence of Olivia and the audience, Jared's fingers ripple the tremolo while this thumb plays the haunting bass melody. When he finishes, the audience erupts with cheers echoing, 'Bravo, bravo'.

"That was excellent Jared," Olivia says, as she retrieves her guitar. "You're extremely gifted. A great classical guitarist once told me, 'If a ten year old can play Recuerdos de la Alhambra beautifully, he is a child prodigy'."

Jared grins. "Oh really, hmm, I guess it's nice to be one."

"Oh yes, Jared. Very nice, now is there a composition you would like me to play?"

"Why yes, Olivia, would you play Sevilla, it's a favourite of mine."

"Yes, of mine too, and you seem to have a talent for picking out pretty things." Olivia pauses to gaze at Jared.

"Oh I get it," he says. "Like picking out pretty tunes and pretty women, eh?

The audience laughs lightly.

"Why thank you, now I'll play Sevilla for you." Her fingers move delicately yet strongly bringing out the exquisite Spanish melody. When she finishes and the applause slips away, she turns to Jared. "You have really added an entertaining segment to my concert. Thank you. You can step down now but I'd like to speak with you and your parents after the show. I'll be autographing my music books and CDs in the lobby."

Jared steps down to a thunderous ovation.

Olivia smiles. "A hard act to follow, folks but I'll do my best."

After the concert Jeff, Sam and Jared stroll into the lobby. There's a row of tables with Olivia's CDs, music books and photographs. Behind the desk are several cashiers handling the sales. Jared stares wide eyed at this feast of music. "I don't have this book or that CD. Can I buy them dad."

"Of course, Jared, this a memorable occasion and a real joy. There's Olivia sitting behind that desk over there."

"Yes, I want her to autograph these."

Olivia's sits calmly flicking a pen while waiting for people to come for autographs. Standing back ten feet or so is a compact group of humans staring at her as if she's some rare creature in a zoo.

Jared walks right up to her. "Could you autograph these please, Olivia?"

"My pleasure, Jared."

Sam and Jeff walk over and after introductions are exchanged, Olivia says, "You are lucky parents to have this charming son. He's extremely gifted and you should try to get him the best musical training you can."

"The problem is, Olivia, he's gifted at everything he does, so we feel that we should let him carry on with his interests until he's old enough to make a choice."

"I suppose I'm biased toward music but it does take a great deal of dedication at the expense of other things to pursue a concert career."

Jeff nods. "Plus the right connections I imagine."

As Olivia signs Jared's purchases, she nods. "Yes, that too."

They are returning home from their marvellous experience in Victoria. As they enter the city limits of Crescent Valley, Jeff says, "It's great to get away from home but it's nice to return. But you know, Samantha, I've never enjoyed myself so much before."

"Me neither, Jeffery."

As they enter the old urban area of town, Jeff drives onto Crescent Valley Way. He pulls up in front of Sam's house.

Sam turns to Jeff and places a hand on his arm. "Why are you stopping here, Jeffery?"

"Well, to let you out, of course."

"Didn't I tell you, I've moved?"

Jeff leans on the wheel and gazes at Sam. "No, you didn't. Where *is* your place?"

"Where's my place? I'll show you where my place is, Jeffery. Just follow my instructions."

By *this* time, Jared has developed an interest and has his chin resting on his arms on the back of the front seat.

Sam gives Jeff's arm a little tug. "Go back to Maple Avenue." Jeff drives there. "Now turn at the next intersection." Jeff does this. "Okay, three blocks and hang a left."

"Why it must be quite close to my place," Jeff says.

Sam nods. "Quite close."

"Well, that will be nice we'll be able to see each other more often than previously."

Sam turns and winks at Jared. "Yes, we will."

"What number is it, Samantha?"

"Well, it's new to me so I've forgotten. You'll have to just drive along the street until I recognize it. Okay, stop right here."

Jeff looks at the place and slowly turns his head. "If *you* plan on living in *that* house *right now*, you're going to have to promise to marry me and stick with me, have you got *that straight*?"

"Yes, sweetheart, I've got it straight." Sam leans over and the two exchange a lasting kiss.

"Yea!" comes loudly into Jeff and Sam's ears. "Plan accomplished."

They get out and walk into the house. "You know, Jeffery, I never even seen all of my new home. Show me please." Jeff leads Sam through the whole house and when they return to the kitchen Jared is sitting at the little table with the odd tear trickling down his cheeks.

"What 's wrong, son, "Jeff asks

"It's…it's…it's just that…I'm just *so happy*, I've got a mom, we've got a family. I knew I had a master plan, but it didn't seem real until we're all here to stay and live."

"Ah, Jared." Sam goes to him and takes him in her arms. "It was a great opus you composed with a beautiful ending."

Big Bang Theory

Bev and I were over at the Sharp's place one night last week. We were knocking a few back pretty good and playing cards. That would be Jack and Tanya Sharp, our best friends. They're around our age, and like us, they've been married for five or six years and have a couple of kids. That's not the reason we're friends. I just thought I'd mention it. This friendship thing got started last year when Jack became sales manager for Crescent Valley Motors. I'm head mechanic there. I took to Jack right away. He's one of those guys that you just *have* to like. Always joking. Hell, he can be a real clown at times… friendly, too. You know, the kind that make good salesmen: clean cut, outgoing, confident as hell. Now you take me, oh I'm a damned good monkey-wrencher or I wouldn't be head mechanic. As for looks, well, you might say I've got the middle-of-the-road looks. Or you might say, my looks are over in the ditch, ha, ha. Yeah, I can be funny too. But I can't hold-a-grease-gun to the way Jack can put a joke across. You know, like he acts them out as he's telling them.

Anyway, Jack's wife, Tanya, now there's a 'looker', if I've ever seen one. Like I mean, awesome! Totally, eh? She's one of those petite chics…well I guess cutie better describes her. You know the kind; a sweet slightly turned up nose and pink dimpled cheeks. Oh sure, I'd love to hop into bed with her. What guy wouldn't, eh? Anyway, I'd never think of doing it. Guess I already have, but then guys do a lot of thinking without doing. But like I said, the guy's my best friend. What kind of a friend would screw around with his best friend's wife, eh? Besides, I'm not the kind of guy that goes out looking for it. After all, I have a wife.

Anyway, we were over at their place playing some cards. They live a couple of 'klicks' out River Road, just beyond where you cross Mosquito Creek bridge, you know, where the road takes that jog. Jack makes pretty good money. You don't own a hobby farm unless you got a few bucks, eh? Of course, it's an old farm and I wouldn't guess he's got it paid for. Tanya's got the place looking awesome, though. Like purple window boxes with pansies hung outside the windows and yellow flowered curtains on the inside. She's got the counter tops covered with orange Formica and the cupboards painted bright red. What taste, eh? And she did the whole-nine-yards herself. I mean really, what a chic.

Anyway, Bev and her were into the gin and tonic pretty good while Jack and I were doing our rye on the rocks justice. We're both rye-men. We know our ryes and we're fussy. Harvest Gold Rye is the way to go. Anyway, the-long-and-the-short-of-it was the four of us were getting pretty well on our way. I'm not saying we were drunk by any means. I'm not saying that at all. What I'm saying is that we were starting to loosen up a bit. You know how it is when you've had four or five good stiff shots of rye. I don't remember exactly how it came up, but Jack said he was over in Sackville on a sales job. He said, he was having lunch at the 'Grin and Bare It' strip pub, with someone he called a potential-sale, when he saw Les Gordon with this young chic. We all know Les and his wife Joan. He sells vacuum cleaners and she's a teller at that bank on the corner of sixth and Maple. They have three kids and live on that rise overlooking the Crescent River right above the rapids there. Anyway, we'd just finished a hand of thirty-one and tossed our cards in the middle of the table. Jack picked them up. It was his deal.

Then Bev picked up her gin and tonic. She took a sip then lowered her glass and said, "I'm disgusted with you, Jack, really, going into a sleazy place like that. Jeff wouldn't go into a sleazy place like that, would you, Jeff?" She paused and looked at me. "No, Jeff wouldn't go into a sleazy place like that."

So what's a guy going to say, eh? So I said, "Not without you."

"Well, you wouldn't catch me dead in one of those places. I mean, how can a girl take off all her clothes with all those guys gawking at her. I mean, really. I couldn't. Could you, Tanya?" She looked at Tanya. "No, you couldn't, Tanya."

"No way," Tanya said. "Basically."

Jack started shuffling the cards. He dovetailed the ends together and with a flourish, bent the deck back so that the cards made that sort of waterfall as they meshed together. He's really slick at it and does it more than it really needs doing; Jack's like that; no matter what he's doing, it's always got to be a show. Anyway, he said, "They make big bucks doing it. I'd do the male strip thing if I needed the money, no problem." Then he stood up, whistled that strip song; I can't remember its name, and swirled his hips as he fanned the cards in front of himself. You know, coy, like the old-fashioned strippers used to do? Of course, they don't do it that way now. Hell, they bare it all now.

Bev looked at Tanya. "Cripes! Guys are all the same, eh? Crude." Then she looked at Jack. "But you wouldn't really, would you, Jack? Jeff wouldn't. I mean Jeff's never even *been* in a strip joi…ah, place…ah, would you, Jeff?" She shook her head and stared into her drink. "No, Jeff wouldn't."

I didn't know what to say, so I said, "If I had enough to show off, I might." When they all laughed, I laughed too, except Bev didn't. She doesn't have much of a sense of humor. So just to keep the talk going I asked Jack, I said, "So what about this chic Les was with? What did she look like?"

"Blond. Shapely. Young. You know the type that married guys look for."

"Is that what you married guys are always doing?" Tanya asked, her voice just sort of took off. "Looking for women to have affairs with? What is this, eh, an ongoing occupation or something? Cripes!"

Tanya sounded more than a little ticked-off with Jack saying this and so he tried to tone the whole shittery down a notch. "I'm talking about the kind of guys that are always checking-out chics. You know the type I mean, the ones who turn to watch a chic's butt after she passes. I didn't mean *all* married men."

"Checking-out chic's butts," Tanya said. "So that's what you guys are always doing, eh, sizing up chic's butts?"

Of course, I do this all the time and Jack does too. What guy doesn't, eh? No harm in looking, I always say. Anyway, Jack laid the deck of cards down and picked up his drink. He raised his glass and looked at it. There wasn't much rye left in it. He swirled the bits of ice that hadn't quite melted yet. "Don't get your knickers in a knot. I was just commenting on how some guys think, that's all."

Tanya rested her elbows on the table and held her glass with both hands. She stared hard at Jack. "So how do you know how these guys think if you don't think that way yourself?"

Jack scrapes his chair back a bit. "Geez! Tanya. Lighten up, eh? I was just casually commenting on a point, for Christ-sakes."

About this time I thought someone should cut in, so I said, "Come on now. Let's face facts here. Our pitooo…you know, that gland…"

"Pituitary gland," Bev said, with a little head toss. She'll do that when she shows off her education. She thinks she's smarter than the rest of us just because she's got a couple of years of college.

I gave her a look. "Well anyway, whatever that gland is called, it's like a fully charged battery: make the connection and Zap, the juice flows. Guys check out chics. Chics check out guys. I mean, let's be realistic, eh? It's the way we're designed. I'll bet any one of us in this room isn't beyond being tempted to…ah, you know, if we found ourselves in the right…I mean in a…well, let's just say a tempting situation. I'm not saying we'd *do* anything. I'm not saying that at all. But you've got to admit, if your being honest, that the urges are there, right? Am I making sense?"

"You're making sense," Tanya said. "We're human…like basically, eh? Some pot or booze and a certain situation and it could happen to any of us…like basically."

Jack got to his feet and sauntered over to the kitchen counter. He poured himself another rye then waved the bottle at me. I nodded. He grinned and brought the 1.5 liter bottle of Harvest Gold over and sat it on the table between us, then picked up the empty bucket of ice and sauntered over to the fridge.

"Not me," Bev said, "You guys can speak for yourselves but I wouldn't do anything. I think love is sacred. Don't you, Tanya? I do."

Tanya didn't answer. She just sat there staring into her drink and swirling the ice every once in a while. She was looking serious but she still looked gorgeous. She always does. Then I said, "But we're talking about sex, here, not love."

Bev knocked back what's left of her gin and tonic and waggled her empty glass at Jack. "More please."

Jack grinned at her. "No Problem, after all I'm the host with the most."

So I said, "Quit bragging."

Jack and I laughed, but Bev and Tanya didn't. Bev was too into her hoity-toity thing and Tanya was still staring at her ice cubes. Then Jack brought the bucket of ice over and picked up Bev's glass.

"Thanks," she said, then she said, "They go together. Sex was given to us as a means of showing our love to our partner. What better way to show your love than to give your spouse the ultimate pleasure in life."

Jack turned from making Bev's drink and grabbed a handful of Kleenex from the box sitting beside the telephone. "That was bee-yoo-tee-ful," he said, then he made like he's crying. Like real sobbing, eh? I mean, you should see this guy sometimes. He slays me. Like at the garage, pirouetting around the grease rack, holding the push broom like it was a chic and singing, 'I could have danced all night, I could have danced all night'. Like the guy can be a real riot at times. Anyway, he brought Bev her drink and said, "You deserve the best of hostmanship for those touching words of tenderness, fair maiden."

Like I was busting a gut laughing at the bugger. I mean, you'd have to have been there and seen the bugger. It was just the way he *did it*. When I settled down, I thought about what Bev had said. "But sex and love are two different things," I told her.

"I'm not saying they aren't. What I'm saying is sex is a gift of love. It is meant to enhance love. Don't you think so, Tanya? I do."

Tanya's still staring into her drink and not saying a word. So I said, "But you can love someone without having sex with them or even wanting to and you can have sex with someone you can't stand."

Bev gave me a *real look*. "Someone you *can't stand?* That's impossible."

So I said, "Guys do all the time. Some of the guys down at the garage take our receptionist, Dirty Daphne, into the washroom."

Bev just looked at me and shook her head. "Cripes, Jeff! Sometimes! I mean, guys are *so* crude. Calling her a name like that."

"Well, she lives up to it."

"Aren't guys crude, Tanya? Guys are *sooo* crude."

Then Tanya pipes in with, "So it's just like another service or repair job with you guys, eh? Or is it more like a recreational sport? Is that it? So I guess you guys were in on this gang splash too, eh?"

I can see right off that she's a little pissed off.

So Jack said, "With Dirty Daphne? Not likely. Besides, I prefer my sex in comfort of my own home, not standing up in the washroom or in the back seat of a car out at some gravel pit."

Tanya gave him a weird look. Her cheeks were getting a little flushed. I wasn't sure if it was from the drink or what. Then she came back with, "But if she was sexy you'd lay her across the back seat of a customers car right there in the garage, eh?"

Jack shook his head. "Oh *sure!*" I think he was a little disgusted with Tanya for saying that. Like Jack's true blue to her.

All this time Bev was gazing into her gin like there was a bug in it. After while, she said in a quiet voice, "Standing up in the washroom? I mean, like really! I just can't imagine that. Can you imagine that, Tanya? And not even *liking her*? I can't imagine that. Jeff wouldn't do that. Would you Jeff?"

Well of course I wouldn't. Like I said before, I'm not that kind of guy. "No way, Jose."

But Tanya, she didn't answer Bev right away. She just reached over and lifted a pack of cigs out of Jacks shirt pocket, tapped one free. Her cheeks dimpled as she took the cigarette in her lips. Then she waggled it at Jack, sort of sassy like. Jack snapped his 'Bic' and waited. But Tanya just looked at Bev and said, "Well, I'd think you would have to like them a bit anyway, like basically, eh?" Then she put the tip of her cigarette up to the flame. She's got these full ripe lips and she puckered them lusciously as she sucked in the flame. I mean she looked awesome, really. Like totally, eh?

"But guys are different," Jack said. "It's more urgent, a more physical thing with men than for women. Don't you think so, sweetheart?"

Tanya jerked her cigarette from her lips and pointed it at Jack. "So how in the hell do *you* know what it's like for women, like basically, eh? You guys act like you're the only one's that have strong urges, that need sex, uh, urgently."

Geez! It wasn't like Tanya. I hadn't seen her so touchy before.

Then Bev said, "But it's true, Tanya. I've read that in psychology magazines. Women are more spiritual oriented with regard to sexual matters than men. Men are lustful."

Of course, I agreed but everyone was getting a bit edgy, so to get off the track, I said, "I read once that during orgasm a person is insane."

Bev shook her head. "That's a crock."

"No," Jack said. "I've read that too."

Then Bev said, "That probably applies to just men. But the point I'm trying to make has to do with people's attitude toward sex. How they feel about it in the preparatory stages and the afterglow. That's where it's at, like the real beauty of the whole thing."

Jack leaned back in his chair, looked up at the ceiling and said, "Prep-a-tory stages. Af-ter-glow." Then turning to me, he said, "I didn't realize that you had such a puritanical chic here, Jeff. And *pro-found*, man, *pro-found*!"

'Puritanical', get that, eh? How does the guy come up with these words? Anyway, we heard a washing machine whir on down stairs.

"Who's that?" Bev asked.

"Oh that's our new roomer in our basement suite," Jack said.

"So you finally got it rented, eh?" I said.

"Finally," Jack said. "Tanya wouldn't rent it to this good-looker that came around last week. Afraid I'd be tempted."

"She was a slut," Tanya said. "Basically."

"A sexy one," Jack said. "But wouldn't you know it, the new one's a dog."

Tanya gave him a quick look and took a quick drink.

"Just listen to him, Tanya," Bev said. "Calling her a dog. Guys are so chauvinistic, you know, like disrespectful of women."

I thought I'd better change the subject, so I said, "I guess the rent money helps, eh?"

Tanya shrugged and said, "Yeah, I guess, but it's kind of like a nuisance, basically eh, sharing the washer and drier with the her. It would be okay if she didn't throw her dirty clothes in with mine. I mean, how careless can you be, eh? I've had to stitch my initials inside the waist bands of my panties so we don't get them mixed up."

Just hearing Tanya mention her panties gave my pituitary gland a good wham.

"Like I told you before," Jack said. "Just wear hers."

"Cripes, Jack," Bev said. "Wearing someone else's under clothes? I can't imagine that. Can you imagine that, Tanya? I can't imagine that."

"In mean like basically, eh?" Tanya said.

Then Jack said, "Why not? They'd be clean?"

Then Bev said, "It's like wearing a dead person's clothes. Gives me the creeps. I couldn't wear someone else's underclothes no matter how clean they were. Could you wear another guy's shorts, Jeff?"

I hadn't ever thought about it so I didn't say anything. Then she said, "No, Jeff couldn't."

I was getting a little bored with this line of talk. Just about then, I thought of this thing that happened to me and a friend of mine, so I said, "Talking about sex, I got to tell you guys about this thing last month when I was grouse hunting with Brad Keeler. We'd driven up Crescent River main. You know that logging road that runs off the highway by the convenience store up there? Anyway, we're several klicks up the road and Brad pulls over and parks his four by four. Said it was good hunting through that logged off area that had grown up in alder shrubs. So to make a long story short, we come out of this clearing. It's a sort of gravel pit off the logging-main. Anyway, we see this pick-up truck parked there. Then through these willows, I see something moving. So I whisper to Brad to be quiet, that I see something. So we sneak over to the bushes and peer over them. There's a bunch of garbage someone has tossed out laying near the bushes; an old mattress, and what do you know, there's this couple buck naked making out on it." I glanced around the table to see the effect this story had on the others. Tanya was just staring at me with this look. Her eyes were like a stray cat I cornered once in a barn when I was a kid. I had to look away.

Then Jack asked, "Did you recognize them?"

"No," I said. "Their butts were toward us so we couldn't see their faces. Anyway, I said to Brad watch this and I fired my shotgun in the air. Well man, you should have seen that chic scramble. Why she damned near clawed that mattress and that guy to pieces before she got herself out from under the bugger. She was on her feet and heading for the truck like a fart in a windstorm, her little butt just a humping it, ha, ha, ha."

"And how *was* her butt?" Jack asked.

So I said, "The cutest little butt you ever laid your eyes on."

"Or hands," Jack said, with a chuckle.

Then continuing with the story, I told them, "So into the truck they jumped without even stopping to dress. Hell, they spun gravel clear across that gravel pit getting out of there."

Jack and I both laughed our guts out, then Jack said, "Did you get a look at who they were?"

"No," I said, "They were moving away from us."

"Where were their clothes?"

"All we found were their underclothes; his shorts and her panties. They must have shucked everything else before they got out of the truck."

Jack chuckled again. "No doubt, nooo doubt. Things got so hot in there they were melting the Vinyl seat-covers."

I laughed and Jack leaned back on the back legs of his chair and laughed at the ceiling. He's got one of those laughs that tails-off with a galloping wheeze like someone choking to death. Of course, he puts it on. A real riot, eh? Anyway, he said, "Too bad you didn't see who they were. I'd love to know. Well, anyway, you proved the Big Bang Theory."

I didn't get it, so I asked, "What do you mean?"

And so he said, "You know how the theory goes; an expanding universe with heavenly bodies retreating rapidly."

We both laughed at that, then if that wasn't enough, he added, "And, thanks to you, they got a big bang out of it."

Well, that last remark had me slapping the table and busting a gut. I mean this guy slays me. What wit, eh? The girls didn't laugh. Of course, like I said, Bev hasn't got much of a sense of humour, anyway. Now I'm not saying Bev doesn't have her good points. I'm not saying that at all. What I'm saying is that she can get a bit uppity at times. You know, the college thing, eh? Now take Tanya, she's got a good sense of humor. That's why I was surprised when she didn't laugh either. She just got up, quiet like, and went over to the counter to mix herself another drink.

"Guys are so crude, eh Tanya?" Bev said, "I just think that was a disgusting thing to do. I'm not surprised you never mentioned that story to me before, Jeff."

Then Jack said, "I'm surprised at you girls. Can't you just *see* that babe scrambling out from under the guy and heading for the truck, her little butt a going hell-bent-for-leather and the guy still ready for business high-tailing it behind her?" Then he looked over at Tanya who's standing with her back toward us at the counter. "Don't you think that was funny, sweetheart?"

Without turning from the counter, Tanya shrugged her shoulders and continued to mix her drink.

Then Jack turned to Bev. "Don't you think that was funny, Bev?'

Bev just ignored him. I could see right off that she was going to go into one of her sermons. She's been like that ever since she took that adult-learning class in psychology at night school last winter. Anyway, she said, "You see. That's what I meant before. You guys are insensitive as to the nature of the underlying nuances of sexuality. What you must understand is that sex is a spiritual and private expression of love and should be looked on with reverence and dignity." Then looking at me, she said, "And, given some privacy. You and your friend should have quietly walked away and never even mentioned the incident again."

Jack looked at me and laughed. "Is that how you saw it?" Then he threw his head back and roared. "Did you see any dangling dignity, revving reverence?"

I mean, the guys got a way with words, eh?

"What did you do with the panties," Jack said. "What about the truck? Did you recognize it? Did you get the license plate number?"

Tanya turned from the counter and looked at me with that look again. Then it hit me like a semi-truck. I remembered Brad picking up the panties and saying, 'Hey, these are like new. I'll give these to Jen.' Then turning the hem out so I could see it, he chuckled and said, 'I'll have to pick these initials out or she'll think I have another girl friend.' I didn't recognize the truck but I noticed that it had a local dealership marked on the tailgate and a B.C. license plate. For a minute, I couldn't think of anything to say. Then I just muttered, "The truck had an Alberta license plate."

"I guess that rules out some local affair then," Jack said, with a chuckle.

"You know, Jack," Bev said. "You guys are worse than us girls. You'd just love for it to have been an affair between some local people so you could gossip about it with the guys at the garage, eh?"

Jack just laughed.

So I said, "Hell! We *all* get hung-up on others affairs because we're all tempted to do the same."

Bev looked at me with that uppity air of hers. "Jeff, really! Sometimes!" Then she looked at her drink. "Well all I've got to say is if everyone took my attitude toward sex, they wouldn't be tempted."

That irked me a bit, so I said, "That's easy enough to say, eh? Like things are *so* easy to say, right? But any one of us in this room could…now I'm not saying we will…would… I'm not saying that at all. What I'm saying is our pitoo…those glands are fully charged and just let someone turn our ignition on and 'vrrrooom' we're burning rubber."

Right then, I shut up, like *right now*, eh? It was like things were all of a sudden so damned quiet I didn't dare interfere with it? I drained my glass and eased it down onto the table. The two melting ice cubes looked as smooth as those two round cheeks heading for the pick-up. There was the quiet meshing of Jack shuffling the cards and the quiet tinkling of Bev swirling her ice. I slipped a look at Tanya. She was looking at me. That frightened look was gone now. Her dimples deepened and her nose wrinkled, like I mean into a gorgeous...a sexy...okay, let's just say, a nice smile. Geez! I don't know. Oh what the hell, eh?

Wait and See

co-authors – Keith Field
and Althea McElheron.

As soon as I heard that Sylvia and Jeremy were going to get married, I decided not to attend the wedding. Sylvia is my best friend and I like Jeremy. Oh God, what will I do; she is sure to ask me to be Maid-of-Honor. But since Brad is Jeremy's brother, Brad will be Best-Man. And we had such a nasty break-up. I didn't enjoy dumping him, like you do have feelings after dating three months. He is so darned immature for being seventeen. I just couldn't take it anymore; after all, I work at The Burger House.

The first thing I said when Jeremy asked me to be Best Man was, 'But Janice is Sylvia's best friend and Sylvia will ask her to be Maid-of-Honor. All Jeremy said was, 'So?' Why try to explain, eh? You see, I hadn't told Jeremy how Janice tried to hang on to our relationship when it was on the rocks. Oh sure, I still have feelings for her. It's just that she was so freakin' picky. 'Do you have to fool with carburetors every Sunday?' 'Do you have to drink beer every Saturday?' As if it was every Saturday, every Sunday. But what really freaked me was the way Janice had 'come on to' that nerd, Zack Skinner, at that party, eh? Okay, so I like Sylvia, okay, and I think that Jeremy and her look cool together. But you know, like being Best Man will be tough, like having to dance with Janice. One thing's for sure though, I'm not about to spoil my brother's wedding. And of course, I'm sure as heck mature enough to handle the situation, I mean like college will do that for you, eh?

Hmm, then again, I don't want to disappoint Sylvia. After all, she has picked out a beautiful cornflower blue gown for me to wear in nicely draping material that clinks in at all the right places, you know, without being too skanky. Oh ya, I just remembered that Brad especially liked blue on me…not that I care what he likes on me anymore.

Now even though I'm a college man now, I still I like my beer drinking buddies. After all, they were my school chums and we've had great times together monkey-wrenching hotrods, going to parties. So what was I supposed to do when Janice put them down? Since I've graduated from high school, I've enrolled in psychology and creative writing at the College. Oh sure, even though my friends still 'hang out' the way they used to, I'm not about to desert them completely; I'm no snob, you know.

I'm standing in the church vestibule surrounded by my Bride's Maids and I simply know Brad is standing nearby with the Ushers. I simply can't resist a quick glance his way. Hmm, not quick enough; he's looking straight at me. For some strange reason, my heart does a little freefall; probably just nerves, after all the responsibility of being Maid of Honor, like really. Darn, he is so handsome and in that suit he just looks gorg…gosh, he always knew the right…uh, buttons… er, to push when we made out. And his kissing was super…now what made me think of those things?

Of course, I'm aware that Janice is pretending to be preoccupied with the Brides Maids. Oh I saw her glance my way so how could I not glance back at her, after all, being in the bridle party we must act friendly. Oh gosh, she looks gorgeous in that powder blue dress with some cleavage showing and long flowing skirt, standing with the other girls; those elongated dimples; oh how I used to love kissing them. Just listen to me, why am I even going there, eh?

As I stand in the bridle party, I'm afraid to look up from the bouquet, and as I hand the Brides ring to the Minister, my hand trembles. Of course, it has nothing to do with Brad's presence; I don't even like him…really…it's the whole ceremony that's making me nervous, I mean, who wouldn't be? I notice that Brad's hand sakes just as much as he hands the Groom's ring to the Minister. This ceremony is simply taking, like forever. Well, it's over now, and Brad, as he's obliged to do, takes my hand and walks with me in the wedding procession up the aisle and outside to the limousine. Just everyone is looking at us. I must smile and nod to them and 'suck it up'.

As Janice steps over, I take her hand, and of course I must smile at her. It will look good to the congregation. She smiles that dimpled smile back. Her hand does feel soft and warm as we walk up the aisle and outside to the limousine. We slide into the back seat together and find that we must snuggle up to make room for the others. I'm mature enough now to handle it. Hmm, ooo, that sweet familiar warmth of her body and that special smell of her...I don't know ...just so familiar and sweet. My God, let it go, guy, it's over.

Oh God, I'm getting goose bumps but it's certainly not cold in here. I smell that familiar aftershave Brad liked to use and the essence of him. Ooo, it turns me on...for Heaven's sake, am I a hopeless case or what? It's over, right? Thank God, the picture taking and the trip to the reception hall is over. Not having to stand with Brad in the reception line helped but now it's time for the obligatory dances. I'm going to freak-out. I'm like a stone statue as Brad takes my hand and we dance but there's something in that familiarity of the scent of his skin as I lay my cheek close to his and the warmth of his body against mine. And his hands, on mine and the other just below the small of my back feels so...I don't know... it just reminds me of how our bodies always moulded into each others so perfect when we...why would I think of that? He's not even my boyfriend anymore or ever will...

Janice feels so nice in my arms, and I'm sure she notices how much more mature I am since I'm college educated. I should tell her. I lean back a little to smile at her. "I thought, Janice, that you might find it interesting to know I'm taking psychology and creative writing at the College."

"Wow, that's great."

My God she looks beautiful in her dress and...shit...what's wrong with me... she'd never take me back if I wanted her too, not that I want her too...it's just... "What are you doing, Janice, since graduation?"

"I well, I've been promoted at The Burger House...that is I..." *Oh God, it sounds so freakin' trivial after what he's doing. And he does sound more mature.*

Hmm, an improvement over fooling with freakin' carburetors. "You know, Brad, Sylvia suggested that I should enrol at the College."

"Good idea I could introdu…well, yes, I think you would enjoy learning there." *For a while I didn't know what to say next so I said,* "Sylvia looks cool, eh?"

"Stunning."

"I kind of like these old songs and dancing this old style of dancing while you hold each other, don't you?"

"Yes, it's so much more romantic."

"Uh, sorry I stubbed your toe, Janice."

"No, no, Brad, it was my fault."

"Mine really, but yes, romantic…I like things romantic, do you?"

"Um hum, soft music with words that are sweet and loving."

"Yes, that's it, isn't it?"

"Exactly."

Then I snuggle up to Janice as much as I dare and say, "Jeremy and Sylvia look romantic together, you know, close in each others arms and snuggling into each other, eh?"

I can feel Brad snuggle in a little closer to me, and say before I can stop myself,, "Snuggling close, yes, feels nice…I mean looks nice." *As the music stops the groom rescues me by approaching me for the next dance.*

Well, since Janice is with the groom, I must dance with the bride. I step over smartly and take Sylvia's hand. The ushers are quick to join in with the bridesmaids and the whole procession circles the floor like a glorified carousel. Hey, I said that rather well, this creative writing course is improving my natural way with words. "You and Jeremy look really cool dancing together. You know, like you are really happy and belong together."

"Why yes, Brad, that's the way we feel; but you and Janice look like you belong together too."

"Hah, oh sure after our messy split?"

"Sometimes things are said in anger that aren't meant, Brad."

"Yes, I know, I feel guilty now at some of the things I said to Janice."

"I imagines she does too, Brad. Don't let her go so easily, she's a keeper guy and so are you."

"What a nice thing to say Sylvia."

"Think about it, Brad, seriously."

I glance over Sylvia's shoulder at Janice dancing with one of the ushers. Hmm, I guess she'll be dancing with them half the night. I may as well, dance with as many brides maids as I can.

Hmm, Brad glances at me, I know he might cause a scene if I dance too much with the ushers just like he did when Zack Skinner came on to me. I'll dance with each just one time or less. There's lots of excuses to use; 'my hairs a mess, bobby pins falling out, I have to phone my folks, I have a cramp in my left foot… better still, abdominal cramps, guys never ask about that one. And so I do this and in no time the guys are all with other girls.

Gosh, Janice is standing over their by herself. "Sorry Lisa, but do you mind, I remembered something I was supposed to do."

"No problem, Brad, see you later."

I better buy her a drink before some other guy gets her. "I'll have two martinis, please."

Ah good, Brad's coming toward me with two drinks. Good, now he won't create that scene I was worried about if I accept the drink. Besides, he'd look pretty foolish standing by himself holding two drinks. And I did say that we could still be friends at the time of our split up.

"Would you like a Martini, Janice?"

Of course, I must take it to be polite. "Wow, a Martini, how utterly considerate of you, Brad."

Janice laughs so I laugh. We're quiet and I don't know what to say, so I say, "I don't have time for beer drinking and monkey wrenching with the guys anymore. You know, it's just that college life puts you in a whole new world."

"Wow, sounds *huge*. I'm going to be enrolling soon."

"Oh good, then you'll fit in with…well, ah, Steve Hunt, I guess you don't know him. He's new here. His parents are new 'profs' at the college and he's in my creative writing class. There's a wine and cheese party at their home on the weekend. There'll be some college 'profs', a jazz band, members of the drama club. He invited me and said I could bring a dat…gir…ah, anyone with me if I wanted."

"Oh wow, like really." *I can't help from gazing right into Brad's eyes and just the way he bites his lip and gazes back at me, oh God, I don't know.*

Damn her, she's making me say this. "I could…you know, like give you a ride…to the party if you'd like to…you know, go…ah, with me."

Oh God, what'll I say. I don't want to make a commitment but to go to a party with college profs…I just can't say no. "That would be nice, actually, if it's not too inconvenient. I wouldn't want to…"

"No inconvenience at all." *Gosh, I'm loosing control of my mature thinking.* "After all, I *do* have to drive right by your place on the way so I might as well, eh?"

"Like why not?" *I cringe at making such a tacky remark.*

So it's settled. Janice has accepted my offer to driver her to the wine and cheese party. So what's wrong with that? After all, she had said, 'Like why not?' Besides, no commitment has been made. I'm certain of that. And it isn't as if we're dating again. It's simply a case of me giving her a ride there. Since she won't know anyone, I'll have to be at her side all night. And of course, she'll need a ride home if she doesn't meet another guy there. Not that I'll ask to drive her home. It's just that there'd be no harm done if I did. Then what? Will that be it? Hmm, if she goes to college like she says she is it would put us in the same world. I'll just have to wait and see. "Would you like to dance, Janice?"

"Sure, why not…ah, of course, Brad. That would be very considerate of you."

I look over at Sylvia and Jeremy. "It must be really like huge, to have the happiness that Jeremy and Sylvia must feel locked together in each other's arms; locked together by love for life, eh, Janice?"

I gaze over Brad's shoulder at the newly-weds. "Oh ya, locked together by love for a lifetime of bliss, eh?" *Hmm, so it's settled. Brad will pick me up and drive me to the wine and cheese party. It's too late to do anything about that now. Not that I want to. This will be huge. It's just that I haven't made any commitments. I could even go home with another guy if I meet one there. Oh my God no, that wouldn't work. What if he made another scene like he did with Zack Skinner, and in front of all these educated people. Oh no, I'm going to have to stick right with Brad all night. Hmm, but that's okay. And of course, go home with him, because I'll need a ride; just have to watch that I don't lead him on, like make him think we're back going steady again. Since I'll be going to college too, I should soon fit in with these educated people that I'll meet at the wine and cheese party. Oh my God, when you think about it, Brad and I will be in a whole new world… together. Hmm, I wonder, eh? Well, I'll just have to wait and see, actually.*

CPSIA information can be obtained at www.ICGtesting.com
Printed in the USA
LVOW082034121012

302516LV00002B/5/P